THE MIDNIGHT LIBRARY

No Escape

Nick Shadow

Hodder
Children's
Books

A division of Hachette Children's Books

Special thanks to Ben Jeapes

Copyright © 2007 Working Partners Limited
Illustrations copyright © 2007 David McDougall
Created by Working Partners Limited, London W6 0QT

First published in Great Britain in 2007
by Hodder Children's Books

1

A Catalogue record for this book is available from the British Library

ISBN-10: 0 340 93024 1
ISBN-13: 978 0 340 93024 3

Typeset in Weiss Antiqua by Avon DataSet Ltd,
Bidford-on-Avon, Warwickshire

Printed and bound in Great Britain by
Clays Ltd, St Ives plc

The paper   s Books
    are
sustai   he

Dare to ~~complete them~~ all!

Welcome, reader.

My name is Nick Shadow,
curator of that secret
institution:

The Midnight Library

Where is the Midnight Library, you ask?
Why have you never heard of it?
For the sake of your own safety, these questions are better left
unanswered. However ... so long as you promise not to reveal
where you heard the following (no matter who or *what*
demands it of you), I will reveal what I
keep here in the ancient vaults.
After many years of searching,
I have gathered the most terrifying
collection of stories known to
man. They will chill you to
your very core, and make
flesh creep on your young,
brittle bones. Perhaps you should
summon up the courage and turn the
page. After all, what's the worst that
could happen ... ?

The Midnight Library: Volume X

Stories by Ben Jeapes

CONTENTS

NO ESCAPE

Emma stepped down from the yellow school bus and looked around the parking lot. A stiff breeze was blowing in from the sea, half a mile away, and tugging her long, dark hair into her eyes. She pushed her hair back behind her ears as she gazed around. Irritating little jigs on a whistle and flute were being played over the speakers. Her friends Abby, Matt and Tyler were in front of her and the rest of the school group milled about between the bus and the entrance to the American Colonies Experience.

The ticket booth was set into a tall log fence, next to a large sign which read: *Welcome to One of the First Settlements in America! Explore Our Nation's History! Travel Back in Time 400 Years!*

Abby was studying the sign. 'That would be kinda cool,' she said, 'if we really did go back four hundred years. Too bad it's just a theme park!'

But it wasn't a theme park, strictly speaking, Emma reflected, it was a reconstruction. The Colonies Experience had been built on the site of a genuine original settlement, but she decided not to say so out loud. She didn't want to sound like a teacher.

'Education disguised as a good time, that's all this is,' muttered Tyler.

'Hey, quit complaining. You're getting out of the math test,' Matt grumbled.

'So are you!' Tyler pointed out.

'Yeah, and I don't mind missing class, but I *do*

mind missing my Tae Kwon Do practice,' Matt said, balling his fists and lashing out with one foot at a passing fly.

Emma had to smile. She would never have pictured short, round-faced Matt as a martial arts expert if she hadn't seen him at it. He didn't really look the part, but actually he was very skilled and she knew he had a shelf full of trophies at home.

'Well, I'm looking forward to it,' Abby said, with a grin.

Miss Barker, who taught their American history class, stepped forward and clapped her hands. 'Line up, people. Line up,' she called.

The four friends shuffled into a rough line with the rest of their year.

'Are you looking forward to this? Emma? Matthew?' Miss Barker asked chirpily. She moved along the line, never pausing to listen for an answer. 'Now, everybody, the park is quite big, so if you get separated from your friends, just make your way back to the entrance. There are plenty of signs.'

'Aren't we old enough to figure that out for ourselves?' Emma whispered to Matt, with a smile.

Matt grinned. 'Hey, I'm just going to look for Tyler's hair in the distance!' he said, laughing.

'At least mine's worth looking for,' Tyler remarked, self-consciously patting his spiky new hairstyle, which Emma actually liked. His hair was a very dark brown, like his eyes. Emma could see that he was proud of his new look.

'Don't stand near any bushes, Emma,' Abby laughed. 'We'll never find you.'

Emma looked down at her jeans and the camouflage-pattern jacket she was wearing. 'It's just in case I want to slip away!' she said, smiling.

Miss Barker produced a group ticket at the desk and they pushed their way on through the turnstile. When they came out on the other side, it really did feel a little as though they had gone back in time – apart from the tarmac paths and the piped music.

They were standing at one end of a street lined

with wooden buildings. Some were log cabins with steeply pointed roofs; some looked more complex, with walls made of planks and boards. Each house stood on its own, surrounded by a small wooden fence which enclosed an area that seemed more like a miniature farmyard than a yard. Chickens pecked at the ground and pigs rooted around for food. It didn't feel like a town, Emma thought. It felt like someone had just cleared a small area out of the wilderness and dropped a community into it, but she realized that that was basically what must have happened when the first European settlers reached the shores of America.

There were lots of actors posing as settlers in authentic period costumes. The men wore three-cornered hats, long coats and rough breeches. The women wore bonnets, blouses and long skirts, their hems trailing on the ground. To Emma, the clothes didn't look particularly comfortable, but the actors wore them as if they were as regular and fashionable as her own clothes. Some of the actors gave the school group a friendly nod as they walked past.

Miss Barker clapped her hands again for attention. 'Right. You've all got the activity sheets. Now, get into groups of three or four and look around at your leisure,' she instructed. 'I want all of you back here, at the main entrance, in two hours. Well, enjoy yourselves!'

The class started to split up and scatter amongst the houses and roads of the little town. Emma, Abby, Tyler and Matt headed for the centre of the village. As they got nearer to the middle, Emma thought that it did start to look more like a conventional town, though it clearly wasn't built around a grid system.

In the very centre of the village was a square of grass with a duck-pond in the middle. Three winding streets led away. One was the street they had just walked along, one seemed to lead away to their right and down to the sea, and Emma couldn't see where the road to their left went. It was strange to see the cluster of houses and the people bustling about without any cars, telegraph poles, satellite dishes or phone lines. As Emma turned in a circle, looking around at the village, she saw two long poles in the distance, poking up above the roof level of the houses. As she stared at them, she realized that they were the two masts of a large sailing ship.

Abby was reading the guidebook. 'Hey, they've even got a harbour area with its own replica of the *Mayflower*,' she said.

That explains the masts, then, Emma thought. She peered over Abby's shoulder at the map of the settlement and noticed that the left-hand road led to a patch of green which was marked as the 'Town Common'.

'This place is kind of neat,' Tyler said with grudging admiration. 'I can almost believe it's real.'

'The real thing would have been dirtier,' Matt pointed out. 'There was no hot water for washing. And most people had fleas.'

'Eeww!' said Abby and Emma together. Abby scratched her hair, which was dark like Emma's, but much shorter. It had once been longer than Emma's and Abby had agonized for ages over whether she should have it cut. She had finally decided to go for it, and Emma had breathed a sigh of relief when the short look turned out to really suit her friend.

They wandered up the street towards the common, then followed the noise of what sounded like two pieces of metal being smashed together. It turned out to be exactly that. A blacksmith was working in a log cabin with one wall completely open to spectators. A crowd of schoolkids had gathered round to watch the blacksmith at work. He was standing by an anvil in front of his shop and pounding away at a lump of metal that glowed with a red heat. His muscles bulged beneath his skin and sweat poured down his face, soaking his hair and streaming into his eyes.

Slowly but surely a shape was emerging. It was as if there was something buried deep within the glowing lump of metal and it was determined to make its way to the surface. The solid, shapeless mass gradually thinned out, turning into a long, wide blade with a curved edge and a point at one end. It was like very slow, real-life computer graphics.

The blacksmith picked it up with a pair of tongs and plunged it into a bucket of water. Gouts of steam burst from the bucket, smelling hot and damp and bitter in the air. Then the smith pulled the cooled metal object out of the bucket and held it up for all to see. If Emma hadn't seen it herself, she would have assumed it was machine-made. Its curves were smooth and steady, and its tip looked razor sharp, and yet with her own eyes she had seen the blacksmith making it in front of her, using nothing but brute strength, a hammer and fire.

Someone began to clap, and soon the rest of the little crowd of onlookers joined in. The smith grinned. 'And that, young squires, is how an honest man makes a good plough,' he said.

Emma smiled at his accent, which was strong and slurred. He was really laying the period acting on thick. The others rolled their eyes.

'Next demonstration is at three o'clock,' he said, which slightly spoiled the illusion. Then he gently ushered the crowd out ahead of him, and pulled a very modern safety shutter down over the front of the smithy. Emma supposed it was to stop small children getting too near the fire.

'Whew,' she said. 'I'm thirsty! Watching all that hard work has really taken it out of me.'

The others laughed.

'How about we head over there?' said Abby, pointing. They had reached the common at the end of the street. It was a huge, wide grassy area, surrounded by woodland. On the other side from the four friends stood a low, long wooden house made of dark planks. It was this that Abby was pointing at. 'The guidebook says it's a café,' she added helpfully.

They all agreed that the café was a good idea and set off towards it.

'I wonder if that tree's real,' Emma said thoughtfully, looking at a large old oak tree that stood on the common.

The others looked at her oddly.

'Well, it definitely isn't plastic,' Matt said.

Emma laughed. 'No, I mean, did they plant the tree as part of the Colonies Experience? Or has it been here ever since the first settlers came?' she explained.

By now they were quite close to it and Emma had to tilt her head right back to see the upper branches.

'It looks ancient,' Matt commented, moving away from the path to examine the tree. 'And oak trees live for hundreds of years. It was probably here before the first settlers even arrived.'

Now that they were almost underneath it, Emma peered around the base of the trunk, looking for a sign like you sometimes saw in parks, saying 'This tree was brought here by so-and-so'. There was certainly something there, sticking out of the ground between two of the tree's gnarled old roots. She looked a little closer and saw, to her surprise, that it was a tombstone.

'Abby, look out!' she exclaimed, but it was too late. Abby had walked in front of the headstone, right over the grave itself in fact.

Abby looked back at Emma curiously. Then her eyes followed Emma's pointing finger to the headstone and she jumped off the grave with a squeal.

The boys hooted with laughter.

'It must be fake,' Matt laughed, while Tyler squeaked and leaped about in an imitation of Abby.

'Ooh,' he squealed, 'it's a scary gravestone!'

Abby looked annoyed.

'Well, it looks real,' Emma said. She leaned closer and squinted at the inscription. The stone was rough cut and very weathered, as if it really had been outside in the wind and the rain for the last four hundred years. Green-grey lichen grew in the cracks and crevices, and the carved letters were

blurred and shallow. 'It says, um, "Herelie . . ."
That's a strange name . . .'

'It's two words,' Matt pointed out. He was also
peering at the writing. ' "Here lie".'

'Oh, yes. "Here lie the w . . . wi . . ." '

' "Here lie the witch children," ' said Matt. '1632.
Wonder who they were.'

'It's a funny place for a grave,' Abby muttered.

'Ah, ye have found the stone!' said a woman's
voice behind them. One of the local guides, an old
woman in a black skirt and bonnet, had come up
behind them. Her face was wrinkled and her lips
were puckered over toothless gums. ' 'Tis not a tale
for Christian ears,' she continued, putting on an act
with wild, staring eyes and an accent even thicker
than the blacksmith's. 'Terrible, they were, the
witch children. Strangers from beyond, with
unholy ways and objects of black magic!'

'Cool,' said Tyler. 'Do they do birthday parties?'
The friends laughed.

'Ah, ye may mock, young squire! But even now

their dark powers live on. Sometimes they may be seen about the town, late at night, though none dare approach them. Sometimes they may take over the soul and mind of a young child—'

'So why is the grave here?' Abby interrupted impatiently. Emma guessed she was still sore at being laughed at by the boys. 'What's wrong with the churchyard?'

'What a strange question, young miss! Bury witches, in God's hallowed turf, among the decent folk of our town? Nay! They are lucky to have a grave at all – out here, alone, so that good people can rest easy.'

'Yeah, whatever,' Abby said. She looked down at the ground she was standing on, and suddenly she grinned and danced a little jig. Emma wondered if she was overcompensating for being scared at first. 'Ooh, look at me, they're making me dance!'

The others laughed and the woman threw up her hands. 'Aye, well, don't be surprised when the bogeyman comes to visit you,' she told them. Then she suddenly reverted to modern English as she walked off. 'And don't forget the gift shop before you leave.'

Emma watched her walk away. Just before she reached the road, she turned back and called, 'Oh, by the way, that grave happens to be real. It was left over from the original settlement.'

The smile vanished from Abby's face and she leaped off the grave with another squeal, which sparked another round of laughter from the boys.

'Come on,' Abby muttered. 'Let's get those drinks.'

The others turned away, but Emma stayed for a moment longer, looking at the headstone and wondering about the witch children. *So, they were real!* she thought. *Not reconstructed, like the rest of the town.* She walked slowly after Abby, thinking that she would borrow the guidebook to see if it said anything about the grave. Who had the witch children been? Probably some special needs kids or children with some sort of illness that the seventeenth century hadn't been able to cope with, she figured. Or maybe they were just children that nobody liked. Poor things. A shiver ran down her spine and Emma was suddenly very glad that she lived in the twenty-first century. Maybe Abby shouldn't have danced on the grave, she thought. It was said to be bad luck and maybe, just *maybe*, the witch children really had been witches!

'Yeah, right,' she muttered to herself, breaking into a run to catch up with the others, who were almost at the café now.

The building stood on small piles of stone, next to a tarmac path that led round the edge of the common. There was a board in one window advertising its prices and a row of wooden benches outside. It was the only building on this side of the common, but you could still hear the piped music faintly.

As Emma caught up with her friends, an icy breeze suddenly whistled past her ears, whipping her hair forwards and into her eyes. 'Ow!' she exclaimed, pushing her hair back from her face.

She heard Matt curse under his breath, as the wind blew a cloud of dust over them and a thundery rumble sounded in the distance.

Tyler put his hand on the door of the café and pushed. 'Sounds like there's a storm coming,' he said. 'Let's get inside. Aargh!' He broke off with a cry as a flash of brilliant white light lit up the day.

For a moment all Emma could see were strange shapes that swam in front of her eyes. It was as if someone had set off a camera flash right in front of her face.

Tyler stumbled in through the door, Emma followed and the others fell in behind her. They all stood in the entrance and blinked, waiting for their sight to come back.

'What was that?' Tyler asked. 'Lightning?'

Matt squinted up at the sky. 'I guess so. It was super-bright though,' he said. 'There must be a real monster storm coming.'

Emma looked up at the sky. It was a clear blue

above their heads, but she could see some ominous-looking clouds away in the distance.

'Well? Are you just going to stand there?' barked a woman's voice.

'Come on,' said Emma. 'We're blocking the entrance.'

They all stepped forward into the café, and then stopped again.

'OK,' Abby announced, 'this is taking the colonial experience too far.'

Emma had to admit that she hadn't been expecting the inside of the café to match the colonial look of the outside. But it did. Instead of a modern, hygienic tea room, this was more like a dirt hovel. Actors in shabby period costumes sat around, drinking out of pewter pint pots and puffing on long, thin pipes. The air was heavily tinged with smoke and the only light came through the windows and from the fire that glowed in the old stone fireplace.

Every one of the actors was staring at the four

friends, and it wasn't in a welcoming way. Just then another chill blast of wind whistled in through the door. Emma shivered.

'Definitely a storm,' Tyler said. 'Come on. We're better off indoors.'

There was a rough-hewn table nearby with a bench on either side, so they self-consciously shuffled towards it and sat down. Emma noticed that the floor was made of bare wooden planks. There were no tiles and no rugs of any kind, and she really, really hoped that the small mouse peeping out of a hole in the wall was some kind of puppet.

A woman in a grubby apron stood behind a counter at the other end of the room, glaring suspiciously at them.

'Do you think this café is just for the actors?' Tyler muttered, as he glanced around. Emma saw some of the men meet his gaze with hostile stares.

Tyler quickly looked away. 'Maybe it's off limits to us.'

'No, the guidebook definitely said it was for visitors,' Abby insisted.

'Maybe the book's out of date,' Emma suggested.

'It's this place that's out of date,' Matt said in a low voice. 'It's *too* real. These people look like they've been wearing their costumes for weeks.'

'They smell like they've been wearing them for weeks, too!' Abby put in.

Emma glanced at one of the men at a nearby table. He met her eye, then looked away from her hastily as if she had embarrassed him. She could see what Matt meant. The clothes looked like they had never been near an iron, and they weren't dirty by being stained or marked. It was more as though years of dirt had become engrained in them.

'So, will you be wanting anything?' the woman behind the counter demanded.

'Oh, um, yes please,' Emma said. 'Could we order some drinks?'

'Aye, you could,' the woman replied unsmilingly. She seemed to be waiting for them.

'Do we go to her?' Abby murmured.

The woman solved the problem for them by rolling her eyes and coming round the counter. She stood over their table.

'And how can I serve your highnesses?' she asked.

Emma really didn't like her tone. 'Um,' she began nervously. Somehow, she didn't want to ask for a menu. There was absolutely no sign of one anywhere, not even in the window, though she could have sworn she had seen one when they were outside. She looked round at the others. 'Lattes?'

One by one they all shrugged and nodded.

'Four lattes,' Emma told the woman.

She got a blank look in return. 'Lattes?' the woman said, sounding bewildered.

'Yes. You know – milk and coffee. Lattes,' Emma repeated hopefully.

'Telling me I know don't make it so,' the woman said flatly. 'We ain't got "lattes".'

'Oh, God,' said Matt. 'OK. Just regular coffee then, please.'

Now *he* got the blank look. The woman was also starting to look annoyed.

'Milk-shake?' Abby tried.

'Maybe just some orange juice?' Tyler ventured. *He* got a scowl from the woman that made him bite his tongue.

'Listen, Master Green Eyes,' she told him. 'I don't have the time for your games. You can have ale like everyone else.'

'Ale?' Tyler repeated incredulously. 'You mean, *beer?*'

'Aye,' the woman said, as if explaining to an idiot. 'Beer.'

'B-but do I *look* old enough for beer?' Tyler asked.

'It's ale, or you can stop wasting my time,' snapped the woman.

'Look,' Abby said, 'if it's all right with you, we'll just sit here and wait out the storm. We won't take up your time.'

'Storm?' The woman peered past them, out of the window. 'What storm?'

Emma followed her gaze, and couldn't believe what she saw. The sky outside was now completely clear – no clouds anywhere. It certainly didn't look like there was a storm brewing.

'But,' Abby objected, 'the lightning, that wind . . .'

Emma could see from the woman's expression that they were about to get another scolding. 'Look, we'll just go,' she said.

'Aye,' the woman agreed. 'That may be best for us all.'

'Gee,' Matt said as he clambered to his feet. 'Service with a smile – not! Maybe you should have a sign saying you only serve booze. That would avoid the confusion.'

But the woman was already turning away.

The others stood up, flushing under the sideways looks of the other patrons.

'And since when were my eyes green?' Tyler asked as they headed for the door.

'Since . . .' Emma began, and then she stopped.

23

She had been about to say 'since never', but suddenly she saw it wasn't true. It was dim inside the café, but she could see that Tyler's eyes were a bright clear green. 'Um, actually they *are* green, Tyler,' she told him. 'Sort of.'

'*What?*' Tyler demanded.

The others crowded round to peer into Tyler's eyes.

'Hey, that *is* weird,' said Abby.

'What colour are they supposed to be?' Matt asked.

'Brown, of course!' Tyler told him.

'Hey, don't get mad. I've got better things to worry about than the colour of your eyes,' Matt protested.

'They're usually a very dark brown,' Emma said. 'And this is a pale green. That's a pretty big difference.'

'Hey, maybe it's some strange atmospheric thing,' Matt said. 'I've heard that things like that can change the colour of your eyes. Maybe that lightning flash was part of it too.'

'Yeah, maybe,' Tyler said, frowning. 'Look, everybody's staring. Let's just get out of here.'

As they turned towards the door, Emma noticed a charcoal portrait on the wall beside it. It had been drawn on what looked like ragged parchment, the size of a poster, and it showed four figures standing together. There were two girls, wearing long, sweeping dresses, and two boys in baggy trousers and thigh-length coats. The drawing was beautifully done, but there was something odd about the figures. Emma moved closer, but even then she couldn't really make out the details of their faces. They seemed smudged, although their expressions were clear enough. The two boys glowered at her, while the girls looked nervous, as if they were poised to run away. Emma thought it looked as though the boys were defending the girls. *Very seventeenth century*, she said to herself.

'Hey, Matt, they can't draw either!' Abby said, pointing to the picture.

Tyler and Emma smiled. They all remembered Matt's less than stellar efforts in art class.

'Oh, my sides are splitting,' Matt retorted.

Emma was still looking at the figures. Abby was wrong. The artist *could* draw, and one of the boys reminded her of someone. Who was it? She stared at the figure thoughtfully.

'Come on,' said Tyler. 'I think my lungs are about to crawl out of my body and die.'

Tyler! Emma realized. *The boy reminds me of Tyler!* Frowning, she looked from her friend to the parchment, and back again. But, suddenly, now she really looked, the boy didn't seem a bit like Tyler, or vice versa. She blinked. For a moment she could have sworn they looked similar.

'Come on, Emma,' Abby said. 'Let's go.'

Emma nodded and followed her friends to the door. But just as they were about to go out, the door opened and an older couple came in. The friends automatically stood back to let them pass, then filed out of the open door.

Emma was the last to leave, and the only one to see the look of sheer horror that flickered across the woman's face when she looked at Emma and her friends.

She grasped the man's arm and crossed herself. 'Oh, saints preserve us, they're back!' she gasped.

The man glared at Emma, and led his companion away. 'They may not hurt us,' he assured the lady, gently. 'We are godly folk.'

Weird! Emma thought. She followed the others outside, wondering what on earth was going on. As she took a grateful breath of the fresh air, feeling relieved to have escaped the pipe smoke in the café, she noticed that the constant background music had stopped.

'OK,' Tyler was saying, 'so what shall we do now?'

'Well, Abby can try not to step on any more graves,' Emma remarked with a smile. As she said it, she glanced at the oak tree on the common that sheltered the gravestone. She frowned. It looked a lot smaller than it had done earlier.

'Oh, yuck!' Matt exclaimed. He was staring at the ground, where he had just stepped in a puddle that was more mud than water. It had stained his bright white running shoes a filthy brown. 'I'm sure that wasn't there before . . .'

His voice trailed off and he frowned as his eyes fell on the path. Emma followed the direction of his gaze. She was sure the track had been tarmac when they went into the café. Now it was just dry earth.

Tyler didn't seem to have noticed anything different. 'Enough with the puddles,' he said impatiently. 'Come on.'

They started walking back across the common towards the village, giving the oak tree and the grave a wide berth.

'Hey, look out, Abby!' Emma warned, just in time to stop Abby from treading in a large cowpat.

'Eeww!' Abby exclaimed. She looked around. 'They're everywhere!'

'And there's why,' Tyler said, pointing. A small herd of cows was wandering about on the common, grazing on the grass. The four humans and the cows looked blankly at each other for a moment, then the cows went back to grazing placidly.

'Shouldn't they be in a pen or something?' Abby asked.

'They probably wandered free in the old days,' Emma pointed out. 'They're just being realistic.'

'You can be *too* realistic,' Abby muttered darkly.

The little group started walking again, carefully, until they reached the end of the main street that led down to the town square. A flock of five or six sheep scattered at their approach.

A light breeze had sprung up, very different from the icy wind they had felt back at the café. It carried a distinctly farmyard smell and Abby screwed her face up in disgust.

'Arr!' said Matt, imitating the 'colonial' actors they had met earlier. 'These be the original smells that came across on the *Mayflower* in 55 BC.'

'First person to get a lecture on colonial farming methods wins a prize,' Tyler added, eyeing a pair of actors who stood by the corner of a house, chatting. One of the men had a pig on the end of a leash. But the chat between the men died away as the friends approached, and the men just stared at them suspiciously.

In fact, as the friends walked further down the street, it seemed increasingly unlikely that they were going to get any kind of lecture from any of the actors. Emma noticed that everyone was staring at them either fearfully or in a decidedly hostile way.

'They're not very friendly,' Abby remarked.

Emma agreed, but the friendliness of the actors wasn't the only thing that had changed. There was something else, though it took her a moment to figure out what it was. 'Is it just me,' she said at last, 'or do the costumes look different?'

The colonial outfits worn by the actors suddenly looked a lot more convincing than they had earlier.

The women still wore long skirts and blouses, but these clothes were plainer in design and colour. In fact, there were hardly any colours, Emma realized. All the clothes were brown or grey or black, with big lace collars and rows of tiny buttons. And everywhere Emma looked, there were a lot more animals.

'Oh, of course!' Abby exclaimed. They all looked at her for an explanation. 'Don't you see?' she said, looking very pleased with herself. 'They must rent this place out to several re-enactment groups. They probably all make their own clothes, so of course some of them are going to look more realistic than others. A new group must have taken over while we were in the café. They're probably on shifts or something.'

'And that's why they're being unfriendly?' Matt asked dubiously.

Emma could see his point. Abby's explanation covered the clothes but not the big change in attitude.

'Maybe we're spoiling their show,' Abby suggested brightly. 'We're probably in the wrong place, that's all. Look, let's find the others. Then we'll know where we're supposed to be.'

'OK, but is this even the right street?' asked Matt. 'It looks different somehow . . .' His voice trailed off as he looked around him.

Emma looked more closely at the houses on either side, and she could see what he meant. The buildings were still made of wood, but they looked more weathered and primitive than she remembered. Many of them seemed to have been patched up with clapperboard and some had thatched roofs.

'Was there a back door to that café?' suggested Tyler uncertainly. 'Maybe we came out another way and this is a different part of the town.'

'I'm sure we came out the same door we went in,' Matt objected.

'Well, it's a theme park, isn't it?' Abby said decisively. 'I bet they just press a button and all the buildings, um . . .'

'Turn inside out?' Matt asked.

Emma was barely listening. Wherever these buildings had come from she was certain she had never seen them before, and yet, as they walked down the muddy street, past the people and the animals, everything felt very *familiar*. Suddenly a flood of memories rushed over her, like a wave.

'I think I know this place,' she murmured.

Matt gave an ironic laugh. 'Yeah, Emma, we were here half an hour ago.'

She shook her head. 'No, no. I mean . . . Look, over there.' She pointed to a house which was a little further down the street, on their right. 'There's a plank of wood nailed to the wall. It covers a hole and—'

'I know,' said Tyler. 'We can see it from here.'

'Yes, but, I . . .' Emma clenched her teeth. 'I already knew it was there *before* I saw it!'

'You probably saw it in the guidebook,' Tyler said dismissively.

Emma looked around her in frustration. She only recognized parts of the town – a flash of something here, a vague memory of something else there. It was like a town she had passed through once with other things on her mind. 'OK,' she said, 'that was a bad example.' But she could see the boys weren't listening now, only Abby was still looking at her. 'Try this,' Emma said. She pointed to a little white clapperboard house. 'That house, over there, I just *know* it's got a stone basin in the kitchen with a big crack running through it.'

'Who told you that?' Abby asked.

'*No one!*' Emma exclaimed. 'But I know I'm right. That's what's so weird. Come and see.'

The girls crossed the road to the house and stood on tiptoes to peek through the window. A woman stood inside with her back to them, washing laundry in the sink. As she moved to one side, the girls caught a glimpse of a dark jagged crack through the basin. Abby and Emma hurried away before anyone caught them spying.

Abby stared at Emma. 'How did you know that?' she whispered uneasily.

They had caught up with the boys, who were pointing triumphantly at a wooden, hand-painted sign at the entrance to the town square that had the name of the village on it.

'See, it's still the same place,' Matt said.

Abby had a sudden idea. 'Hey, wasn't there that website with the whole virtual village on it?' she said eagerly, looking at Emma. 'Remember? You could walk around it and everything. That must be why you think it all looks familiar.'

'Oh, yeah, I remember,' Tyler put in. 'Cool. Problem solved.'

The others seemed happy to agree, so Emma didn't want to upset them by saying what came into her head, which was, *What, the virtual village had a house with a cracked sink in it?*

'OK,' she said instead. 'Let's have a real look around. Let's join in. I mean, maybe that's why no one looks very friendly – they go to all this trouble to do a convincing re-creation for us and we don't seem interested.'

'All right,' Tyler agreed.

They all walked on into the square. Like the street they had just come down, it wasn't quite like Emma remembered it. There were more people here. But one man in particular caught Emma's eye because he wasn't going anywhere. In fact, he was just standing there, on the far side of the square, looking at them.

'Let's ask these guys here,' Tyler said, pointing to a pair of carpenters, maybe a father and a son, who were working on one side of the square. 'Maybe they'll start telling us all about traditional woodworking techniques.'

The two woodworkers had a wooden bench set up next to a house. They were planing a length of wood. It seemed to be a two-man job – one pushed, the other pulled, and the plane skimmed over the surface of the timber, shaving off a thin sliver of wood with every stroke.

The four friends wandered over to watch. Emma remembered the blacksmith's cheerful presentation earlier on. This was just as impressive to watch, in its own way – a pair of ordinary men using nothing more than their own muscles and a basic tool to create something useful.

'Hi,' said Matt. 'How are you guys doing?'

The older carpenter looked up, then pointedly looked away again.

'Of course, we don't want to interrupt,' Abby put in politely.

The younger man lifted his head then and opened his mouth as if to speak, but the older man caught his eye and gave a slight shake of his head. Immediately, they both looked back at their work and started to plane just a little faster.

'Fine,' said Tyler, and Emma thought he sounded hurt. It had been his idea, after all. 'You guys have a real nice day, then . . .' He turned away, and Emma heard him mutter, '. . . and try not to drop dead or anything, 'cos that would be too bad!'

The friends had even less luck with the next person they approached. It was the man they had seen earlier with the pig on a leash. He simply hurried past them, murmuring, 'No, no, no,' under his breath. It wasn't clear to Emma if he was saying it to them or to himself. Or maybe he was talking to the pig.

A woman rounded the corner of a house with two children. The moment she saw the friends, she turned round and bustled the children back the way they had come.

'Hey, we paid money for this!' Abby protested out loud to no one in particular. 'Well, the school did.'

Matt grinned. 'I know Ty smells,' he said to the girls, 'but I didn't think it was that bad.'

Tyler jabbed him in the ribs.

Emma wondered whether she should point out the fact that the townspeople weren't just being unfriendly. They also looked *afraid*. Except for one man – the one Emma had seen earlier, watching them. Throughout all their attempts to interact with the townsfolk he had just been standing and observing.

He stood at the top of a small flight of steps that led up to the porch of the largest building in the square. The building was wide and tall with a small tower at one end. The man was still regarding Emma and her friends gravely. His face was lined and his hair was grey, but he looked as if he could be friendly when he chose. He wore the same style of three-cornered hat and knee-length woollen coat as many of the other men, but the clothes appeared neater and better looked after. They seemed to Emma to have a touch of extra quality.

'Maybe we should try him,' she suggested, indicating the man at the top of the steps.

'Right,' Abby snapped impatiently. 'One last try to be polite, then I'm heading for the exit.'

'Me too,' Tyler agreed. 'Go on, Emma.'

Emma walked over to the man, feeling slightly

nervous, while the others trailed behind. She wondered what she should say first, but as it turned out he saved her the trouble.

'Greetings to you, young friend,' he said. He hesitated, then suddenly held out a hand to her. Emma shook it, just as hesitantly. 'I am Obadiah Johnson, the mayor of this town,' the man went on.

And as he spoke, Emma felt that this man was familiar. But at the same time, she also knew that she had never met him before. Was he a famous actor perhaps? She peered at him. He didn't *look* familiar, but his voice rang bells. *Maybe he just does voice-overs*, she thought.

'Have you travelled far to be here?' Obadiah asked.

'Oh, yeah, thousands of miles,' Matt said, with a shrug at the others.

A smile suddenly appeared on Obadiah's face, but Emma thought it looked insincere, as if he had just that moment decided a smile would be a good idea. 'Then you must come in!' he said. 'You will be tired and in need of refreshment.'

'Well, he got that right,' Abby murmured. Emma agreed – they never had got their drinks in the café, after all.

Abby squinted up at the mayor, her face curious. 'Do I know you from somewhere?' she asked. 'I'm sure I recognize you.'

'Our community is not large,' he agreed. 'Doubtless we have met before. Please, come, enter . . .' Obadiah stood aside and gestured for them to walk up the steps and into the building.

Emma hesitated at the door and glanced back at him.

He smiled. 'Please,' he said, and gestured again. So in she went, thinking that Obadiah only ever seemed to smile when someone was looking at him. She took one last look back outside, and saw Obadiah staring out across the square. As she watched, he gave an almost imperceptible nod to the townspeople who had gathered in the street.

Silently, the people start to walk towards the building.

Emma was feeling very uneasy. She turned quickly back to her friends to see if they had noticed anything strange about Obadiah, but they were all looking around the room they were now in.

It was large and square, and must have taken up most of the ground floor of the building. There were rows and rows of low wooden benches. They looked dark, unpolished and uncomfortable. There were two large, glass windows in each wall – and, somehow, Emma just knew that these were the only glass windows in the town. The walls themselves were plain and unadorned with anything other than a quick lick of white paint. Facing the benches was a wooden stand supporting a large black Bible.

'This looks like a courtroom,' Matt murmured.

'Or a church,' Abby said.

'It is both,' Obadiah said behind them. 'The

Lord's justice and the justice of the community are as one.'

Emma was certain that this hadn't been in the virtual village on the website, so she shook her head, trying to work out *why* she felt as though she had seen it all before . . .

And suddenly there was a stabbing pain in her head, and she felt desperately short of breath. Even though Emma knew she was standing in the courtroom with her friends, at the same time she felt herself running down the dirt road leading to the common, a long skirt catching at her legs, threatening to trip her, while her heart thundered in her chest. Her breath came in short, sharp gasps, and she felt unbelievable terror. A great crowd of people were in pursuit, and her friends were with her, also running.

The Emma that was fleeing for her life risked a glance over her shoulder. Some of her pursuers were no more than a few feet behind, and their faces were contorted with hatred. Some waved clenched fists, others gestured with scythes and axes and knives. All of them seemed determined that Emma and her friends should *die*.

Emma shook her head and clutched at one of the benches as the pain in her head, and the vision, faded. *Wow! Where did that come from?* she wondered. For a moment she had felt like two people, both at the same time!

'Hey, looks like we finally have company,' said Abby as the front door opened again. Obadiah stood back to let the people of the town file silently into the room. There were a lot of them and in very little time the benches had filled up. The men sat at the front, the women and children at the back, and the friends found themselves pushed further and further into the room.

'So what's this?' Tyler asked. 'Are you all going to pray or something?'

Emma's gaze fell on a scythe that one of the men was carrying. *Why would anyone bring a scythe to church?* she asked herself. And as she wondered about that, she suddenly realized that it looked horribly familiar. Her gaze moved up to the face of the man who held it. He was unshaven, with dark, curly hair, and he stared impassively back at her. But the thing that terrified Emma was that *it was the same man she had seen in her vision*.

'Oh, my God!' she gasped, looking quickly around the room. She recognized a blond man, his eyes fixed on her. In her vision, he had been carrying a knife. And then she spotted it, tucked into his belt.

'This isn't right!' Emma whispered urgently. 'This isn't right at all!'

'That's for sure,' said Matt affably. 'There isn't a McDonald's for miles.'

'No!' Emma protested. 'It's more than that. It's worse than that, Matt. *Matt?*'

Her friend was standing in front of one of the windows, which meant that the light was behind him and his silhouette showed clearly. And for a moment it was a different boy who stood there. Emma blinked and shook her head, and when she looked again she saw that it was just her friend Matt, standing, looking at her – but was his nose a bit more pointed than usual?

'What's going on?' Abby asked.

Emma was wondering the same thing, not least because Abby's hair looked noticeably lighter and longer than usual. It reached almost down to her shoulders. And Tyler's eyes were still that extraordinary green . . .

Emma was about to ask Abby about her hair, when Matt turned to Obadiah.

'Uh, Mr Johnson?' he called. 'About those refreshments . . .'

One of the men at the front of the crowd suddenly shot out a hand and grabbed the sleeve of Abby's coat.

'What is this?' he hissed. 'What devil's cloth?'

'Hey, leave me alone!' Abby exclaimed, snatching her hand back and rubbing her arm.

The crowd, which had been so eerily silent at first, began to murmur.

'OK, so it's not wool,' Abby went on, 'but we're not part of your stupid re-creation, are we?'

'What strange words does she say?' someone whispered. The murmur of the crowd grew louder. A lot of people seemed to be pointing out the clothes that the four friends were wearing.

'No Christian wears designs such as those,' Emma heard one man say fearfully, his eyes fixed on Matt's T-shirt with its Tae Kwon Do symbols.

'Aye, no Christian, but witches may,' said another.

'Witches!' Emma exclaimed. 'They think we're witches!'

Tyler snorted. 'Hey, newsflash just in, guys. This is the twenty-first century and we don't fear witches.'

'You even deny the year of our Lord?' a man shouted angrily. He grabbed Tyler's collar and twisted it, forcing the boy to his knees. 'This is the year of our Lord, sixteen hundred and thirty-two, and don't you forget it. We will have none of your devil's calendar here!'

'Ow! Let me go!' Tyler shouted. 'This isn't funny!'

No, said a small voice at the back of Emma's mind, *this* so *isn't funny, because here they kill witches, they murder them. And any moment now they're really going to turn on us and we'll be running for our lives, just like I saw in that vision . . .*

Abby batted at the man holding Tyler with her fists, but he was large enough not to pay any attention. 'This isn't the seventeenth century!' she screamed. 'We've had enough of your pretending.'

It was just then that the alarm on Matt's watch chose to go off, tinnily playing the *Star Wars* theme in electronic beeps. The man holding Tyler leaped back, and Tyler quickly clambered to his feet. The crowd cowered while Matt struggled to switch the alarm off.

'Need we any more proof?' bellowed a voice Emma recognized. She turned to see Obadiah standing at the back of the room. He pointed an accusing finger at the friends. Gone was his former polite friendliness. His eyes were fixed on Matt's watch. 'They are witches!' he hissed.

'Witch!' someone whispered.

And then others gradually took up the refrain, until the whole crowd was crying: 'Witch! Witch! Witch!'

'Proof!' Obadiah declared. His face split in a smile of unearthly satisfaction. 'Proof that these are sons and daughters of the devil – just as we have always known they were.'

The friends cowered as the people leaped to their feet and surged forward, but the ones at the front still held back a little, looking warily at the friends. They seemed to lack the courage to draw close enough to actually touch the four, but Emma could see their courage building with every repetition of 'Witch!'

'These people are *insane!*' Abby exclaimed. 'Let's get out of here.'

'Through that bunch of crazies?' Tyler asked, pointing at the oncoming crowd.

'No. Through the window,' Emma said, turning to the window behind them.

Tyler nodded and picked up a wooden stool to knock out the glass, but as he did so, part of the crowd surged forward with an angry shout and cut off their escape.

'You'll not escape us! Witches!' one man yelled.

Emma could see that they were now surrounded. Tyler looked from the stool in his hands, to the crowd, to the window beyond them. Emma could see the wheels turning in his mind. He must have known he couldn't fight his way through so many people.

'OK. I've now officially had enough,' Matt said through gritted teeth. And then he smiled and bowed at the man nearest to him.

The man paused and frowned, obviously taken aback by this strange behaviour.

'Oh, yeah,' Tyler murmured with a wicked

smile. They all knew what it meant when Matt did this, and in a moment the crowd would find out too.

'*Hai!*' Matt screamed as he leaped up and lashed out with his foot, connecting with the man's chest. The man staggered back as all the air was knocked out of his lungs.

Matt landed in a fighting stance and part of the crowd drew back in horror. Apparently they weren't expecting the witches to use Tae Kwon Do.

'Score!' Tyler shouted triumphantly.

But Emma blinked and shook her head, because, for a moment, Matt had again looked like a completely different boy – someone taller and more sinewy.

And then, suddenly, even while she knew she was still in the courtroom, she could feel herself somewhere else again.

She was watching, helplessly, as the furious mob bore her friend to the ground. Screaming, kicking and swearing, he was picked up, his thrashing legs and arms held tight and a foul rag stuffed into his mouth to silence him.

'*Now*, Tyler!' Matt shouted, bringing Emma out of her vision and back to the courtroom fight surrounding her.

'Right!' Tyler lifted the stool in his hands and rammed its legs into the glass of the window. The glass shattered with a deafening *crash*.

'Stop them!' yelled someone. And a man ran towards Emma and Abby, but suddenly Matt was in the way. Another blow from him sent the man flying back into his fellows.

'It is the devil himself who fights for them!' Obadiah bellowed, still safe at the back of the crowd.

'Out! Get out!' Matt shouted.

Emma and Abby were already on their way, clambering on to the bench and ducking low through the window to avoid the jagged spikes of glass that were still stuck in the frame. They jumped out with Tyler right behind them.

A furious roar went up from the mob inside when they saw that the friends were escaping. Matt had time for one more strike at a would-be assailant, and then he lunged through the hole in the window in one flying leap.

'Run,' he gasped, and no one needed any further telling.

Emma risked one glance behind her as they pelted across the square, sending a couple of chickens flapping and squawking out of their way. She saw the mob beginning to pour out of the door of the courthouse. Then she looked ahead, and considered where she and her friends were headed. Instinctively, they had fled back up the main street, towards the common. But Emma thought of her earlier vision and remembered how her friend had been captured.

'No, this way!' she called, veering towards the square's other exit. It was the street they had come down when they had first entered the Colonies Experience.

And so Emma led them all back towards the park's main exit, until they reached a crossroads and staggered to a halt.

'Which way?' Tyler moaned, panting.

Emma glanced around frantically. The town no longer bore any resemblance to the reconstructed village she remembered. It was as if whatever strange transition had been taking place was now complete.

'We'll have to just keep going,' she urged. 'The town can't go on for ever.'

A cry of 'Catch the witches!' sounded behind them and made the friends stagger forward into a run again. Emma glanced back to see that the crowd was flooding out of the square now, not running, just walking purposefully towards her. Emma thought their steady march made them look even more frightening, as if the crowd knew that the friends had nowhere to run, so they could afford to take their time.

Emma ran on and on and, sure enough, she soon

reached the end of the street, and the end of the town with it. Back in the twenty-first century, she knew this had been the Colonies Experience car park. Now it was just a thin strip of open land, with woods beyond. The street turned into a muddy path that led into the trees. Just before the trees the path crossed a small, windy stream via a wooden bridge.

'My side hurts,' Abby moaned, clutching at her waist as she ran.

'And my feet,' said Matt.

Emma shared the feeling. Her trainers were more for show than for actually doing any running.

'Come on,' Tyler said. 'Maybe we can lose them in those woods.' He took the lead, running across the open strip of grass and then over the bridge. The others followed, their feet thumping hollowly on the wooden planks.

Then Abby caught her foot in a gap between planks and screamed as she pitched forwards. She crashed into the rickety rail of the bridge, and for just a moment her head and shoulders lurched dangerously over the side. Then Emma managed to catch her arm and pull her back.

As Matt and Tyler gathered round to help Abby, Emma saw her eyes fall on her own reflection in the water below.

'That's not me!' Abby exclaimed, pointing. She brushed her hair back from her eyes, something she hadn't had to do since she got her long hair cut, and squinted in confusion up at her fringe. Then she looked back at the reflection and her voice rose. 'That's not *me*!' she said again.

Emma stared at her friend and realized that she no longer looked like Abby at all. Her short, practical hairstyle was gone. Now her hair hung past her shoulders in a long, blonde sweep.

Emma turned to look at Tyler's green eyes and Matt's pointed face. She knew that her friends hadn't always looked like this, and yet these new features looked so natural and their new faces still seemed so familiar. Emma frowned as a new thought occurred to her: if her friends had changed, then what about her?

Very reluctantly, Emma looked down at her own reflection – and saw a complete stranger looking back. Instead of her shoulder-length dark hair, this girl had shiny red locks pinned up on top of her head. As Emma stared in shock, she saw that her real reflection was still there too, but it seemed to be merging into this new one. She could still see her camouflage-pattern jacket, but she could see the cloak and long skirt worn by the other girl. Even as she watched, Emma could see the red-headed girl's image growing stronger and her own reflection fading.

Saints preserve us, they're back! That was what the woman in the café had said when she laid eyes on the four friends. And as Emma thought back to the café, she remembered the charcoal portrait on the wall, and realized that she and her friends were beginning to look like the boys and girls from the picture.

'We're them!' she exclaimed. 'We're becoming the witch children!'

The others looked at her blankly.

'Which children?' asked Abby.

'The *witch* children!' Emma insisted. 'The ones they buried beneath the tree. This isn't a reconstruction. This really is 1632 and the townspeople really are chasing us!'

She remembered the lightning flash as they had entered the café. Had that been when everything changed? It was certainly when everything started to get weird, she thought. Her heart pounded. It was like every nightmare she'd ever had was coming true. They weren't just miles away from home, they were *centuries* away from everything they had ever known. 'We've turned into them, somehow,' she murmured. 'Their spirits are taking over, or something . . .'

'We'll worry about that later!' Matt snapped, looking nervously over his shoulder.

Emma followed his gaze and saw that the crowd

had just come into view. Obadiah was at the forefront, clutching his Bible in his hands and pointing at the friends.

'Right now, we've got to keep running!' Matt said grimly.

Spurred on by Obadiah, the crowd surged forward with an angry roar. The friends raced on again, over the bridge and towards the line of trees that loomed ahead. Soon they were in among the trees, twigs scratching at their faces and brambles catching at their legs.

'Do you think we can lose them in here?' Matt gasped breathlessly, slowing to a halt.

'We . . . could . . . climb a . . . tree,' Abby panted. 'You know. Hide . . . in the . . . branches?'

'Can we get up there?' Emma asked, looking at the nearest tree. Its lowest sturdy branches were a good six or seven feet from the ground.

'Maybe not all of us,' said Tyler, following her gaze. 'But we can all help each other.'

Emma thought it was a good idea. They couldn't

keep running for ever. Somehow they needed to try and throw their pursuers off their trail.

Abby scrambled easily up into the branches of an oak, while Tyler boosted Matt up behind her. Emma could hear the sound of the crowd drawing nearer.

'Get as high as you can,' Tyler hissed to Matt and Abby, 'and then keep still!' A small flurry of twigs and bark drifted down as the two in the tree tried to do as he said. 'Come on, Emma. I can help you up too.'

'There's no time,' Emma objected. 'We have to find a bush or something . . .' She looked around desperately.

'Right. You take that one over there,' Tyler said, pointing to a large, leafy bush growing at the base of a beech tree.

'There won't be room for both of us!' Emma protested.

'Exactly. So I'll find somewhere else. *Go on!*' Tyler urged.

Emma really didn't want them to split up, but she could hear the crowd crashing through the trees now, so she dived beneath the bush, and immediately found that it was a good choice. Beneath the leaves there was a small hollow in the ground, and it was full of twigs and dead leaves so that she could burrow right down into it. Lying there, half covered and absolutely still, she felt pretty sure she would be hard to spot.

Tyler wasn't having as much luck. He ran across her field of vision, then back again. She heard the rustling of leaves and branches as he unsuccessfully tried out several hiding-places. Eventually she saw him take a final, desperate dive into a patch of long dry grass, where he lay absolutely still. Only a few moments later, the crowd was upon them.

The townsfolk had slowed down again now, and they were walking purposefully as they peered around for wherever the friends might be hiding. It didn't take them long at all to find Tyler. A couple of them almost fell over him in the tall grass. There was a triumphant shout from one of the men, and Tyler leaped up like a startled bird. He put his head down and dived between the two men, but a third swung the handle of his axe at Tyler as he ran by. It caught him on the head and he fell face down in the dirt, where he lay as if dead.

Emma bit her tongue to stop herself from screaming out loud. Some of the men cheered and a couple of them picked up Tyler's limp form, holding him roughly beneath the arms. Emma stared hard at Tyler, trying to work out whether he was still alive. He seemed to move, but she couldn't be sure whether it was just because of the way the men were handling him.

'Now,' said a familiar voice, above her, almost making Emma jump. A pair of feet came into view and stopped right in front of her eyes. Fortunately, their owner, Obadiah Johnson, had his back to Emma as he addressed the crowd. 'One witch down, three still to find. Look very closely, brothers. Who knows what forms they might be able to take? They may no longer appear human, but the Lord will grant you the power of discernment.'

If only! Emma thought bitterly. *I wish I was a witch and could turn myself into a tree, or a squirrel.*

But she was very grateful for her camouflage coat as the crowd spread out, peering into bushes and poking up into trees with their pitchforks and sticks. Emma shot a quick look at the tree that hid Abby and Matt, and fought back a gasp of horror. One of Matt's trainers was sticking out of the foliage!

'Ah! I see a little bird!' Obadiah shouted.

The crowd let loose bloodthirsty cheers and Matt quickly pulled his foot up into the tree, but the damage was done. Three of the taller men swung themselves easily up into the branches and climbed up to where Emma's friends were hiding. Through the leaves Emma couldn't really see the struggle, but after a moment a screaming Abby was flung out of the tree. She plummeted towards the ground to be caught by a couple more of the townsfolk at the last moment.

'Ye'll not cheat the Lord's justice that way!' Obadiah announced, giving Emma the distinct impression that they hadn't caught Abby out of pity.

Matt was still putting up a struggle, but up in the tree his Tae Kwon Do was of little help. Eventually, he was knocked off his branch and he fell, only to catch another branch as he tumbled past it. He dangled by his hands, but as he tried to swing his legs up again, one of his attackers stamped his boot down on Matt's fingers. Matt shouted with pain and dropped to the ground.

'Only one more to go . . .' Obadiah said happily, as Matt and Abby were dragged off after Tyler. Unlike Tyler, Emma noted, they were still very definitely alive, for they were kicking and screaming all the way.

'Where are you, witch girl? Where *are* you?' Obadiah said in a singsong voice. Then his tone changed. 'Ah! I see you!' he snapped.

That made Emma jump just enough to make the leaves covering her rustle. Fortunately the townspeople were making so much noise of their own among the leaves and twigs of the forest that no one heard her. Emma forced herself to stay put and keep still. Her instinct had been to make a run for it when Obadiah said he could see her, and that was obviously what he had wanted, but she wasn't going to be that stupid. Now she thought about it, she realized he had been looking in completely the wrong direction to have really seen her.

'She'll be past our town boundaries by now,' someone murmured. 'We can leave her to the animals.'

'Aye,' Obadiah agreed, though he sounded reluctant. 'I would have preferred to present all four to the Lord's justice. But His will be done. Come, let us deal with the others.' He stalked off through the undergrowth, and, one by one, the townsfolk followed after him. The woods fell silent except for the sound of the wind through the leaves and the twittering of the birds.

Run away! Run away! Emma thought. But she had no idea where to go. And more importantly, she knew she could never live with herself if she abandoned her friends. She decided that she would do what she could to rescue them.

Making as little noise as she could, she inched forward, out of her hide-away. Then she stood up, keeping her eyes peeled for the slightest sign of people. She brushed herself down to remove the debris of twigs and leaves that clung to her and then set off back to the village.

She had gone about five steps when Obadiah stepped out from behind a tree in front of her.

'We hoped you might join us,' he said calmly, his eyes alight with unholy glee. 'Take the witch.'

Emma turned to flee, but two more men had stepped out of hiding-places behind her. They seized her and pulled her to the ground.

'Bind her,' Obadiah ordered. Emma cried out and

struggled, but they rolled her over and pushed her face into the ground so that she couldn't breathe. Her hands were tied behind her back with rope, and then she was hauled roughly to her feet.

One of the men leaned forward so that his face was almost right up against hers. His breath smelled like rotting meat and his teeth were black with decay. 'Do we bind your feet too, witch, or do you walk with us?' he snarled. Emma didn't get a chance to answer. Someone shoved her hard in the small of her back, and she staggered forwards. Her arms were grabbed and she was marched back the way she had run earlier.

What are they going to do with us? Emma wondered. She tried hard to remember what people had done with witches in the old days. When they came to the stream, she had a sudden panicked memory that they used to test witches by drowning them. But the stream wasn't that deep, and anyway, Obadiah seemed to have decided that she didn't need to be tested.

She was taken across the field and down the street to the town square. And then her heart leaped, because there in front of the courthouse were her friends, alive and sitting on the ground with their hands tied behind their backs – even Tyler, whom she had last seen lying so still she had thought he might be dead. They half smiled when they saw her.

'Hi, Emma. You should have run,' Tyler said. His voice trembled and Emma guessed he was forcing himself to be brave. The blow from the axe handle had left a massive bruise on the left side of his face and his left eye was swollen shut.

If he was going to be brave, Emma decided, she would be too. 'Well, someone had to get you out of this mess,' she said, with an attempt at a grin.

'Maybe they'll put us in the stocks,' said Abby hopefully. 'Hey, Matt, think you could bust out of some stocks?'

'I'll bust *something* the moment they untie me,' Matt growled threateningly.

Obadiah stood in front of them. 'On your feet, witches!'

Emma was still standing. No one helped the others, who had to struggle to their feet with their hands behind their backs. Emma looked around for some stocks, but she could see no sign of any. It looked like Abby's hope was misplaced, and from the grim looks on everyone's faces, she suspected something much nastier was in store.

They were led round the side of the courthouse, and what she saw there made Emma stop in her tracks. There was a huge stockpile of wood and sticks heaped up in the yard at the back of the courthouse. At one end a single, solid stake had been plunged into the ground, and around it were piled clusters of sticks ready for a bonfire. The stake was scorched and charred from previous fires, and the ground was covered in ash. Clearly the bonfire had been used before.

Suddenly, Emma found herself being lifted up.

She squirmed and struggled, but there was nothing she could do except scream. Her friends were being carried too.

'Oh, no! NO!' Abby shrieked. 'Please!'

'No!' It was a boy's voice Emma heard this time, and it took her a moment to realize that it was Matt's. All his bluster had disappeared. 'No, not the fire!' he wailed.

'We're *not* witches!' Tyler bellowed. 'We're *not*! Do we *look* like witches?'

But he didn't even look like Tyler any more, Emma thought. The transformation that had begun with his eyes was now complete. His head was narrower and his jaw more prominent. When Emma looked at him, she saw a stranger where her friend had been. And yet she knew he was Tyler, just as she knew that the girl with the long, blonde hair was Abby and the tall boy with the pointed nose and the square chin was Matt.

She couldn't see herself, but she could guess what she looked like now. All four of them had become exactly like the children in the drawing on the wall of the café.

Tyler was still trying to convince the townsfolk that they had made a mistake. 'We're not witches, I mean, heck, we're not even the *kids* you think we are!' he shouted.

Abby and Matt had given up on trying to persuade the mob that they weren't witches. They were just sobbing and weeping and begging for their lives. Emma was surprised to find that she felt quite calm. Somewhere deep inside her she was sure there was something that screamed with outrage and horror at what was happening. But all she knew was that in her conscious mind she felt eerily at peace. She wondered if it was shock, or maybe it was just denial – maybe she just couldn't believe that here, in this poky little yard, she and her friends were about to be burned alive at the stake.

The friends were passed from man to man, until they were lashed to the huge stake in the middle of the bonfire. Emma groaned as the rope was pulled so tight about her waist that she could barely breathe.

The man who had tied it grinned in her face. 'Not to worry, witch,' he spat at her. 'It won't bother you long.'

Obadiah stood on a small box, and held up a parchment from which he began to read aloud. 'Know ye, that upon this day in the year of our Lord 1632, the four witch children, for their heresies too many to number, for their transgressions in the ways of the Evil One, for their renunciation of the waters of their baptism and for their denial of the grace of our Lord – their guilt being made evident in their attempt to flee justice, in their strange ways and in the words from their own mouths – are to be put to death by burning, in accordance with the just laws of our community and the commands of Holy Scripture.'

The crowd cheered as Obadiah folded up the parchment and fixed the four friends at the stake with a look of glee. 'Thou shalt not suffer a witch to live!' he proclaimed.

Emma saw a man coming through the crowd, holding a smouldering stick in one hand and shielding the flame with the other. He touched the stick to the tinderwood at the foot of the bonfire. After a moment, white smoke started to drift out of the dry kindling, and the first tentative orange flame lapped at the sticks. The man nodded with satisfaction and moved around the fire to repeat the procedure.

'Burn!' someone shouted. 'Burn!'

The crowd eagerly took up the chant. 'Burn! Burn! BURN!'

The flames were clearly visible now, and Emma began to feel their heat. At first it was pleasantly warm, but in no time at all it began to grow harsh and scorching against her face. She could feel drops of sweat running down into her eyes, and bitter smoke caught in her throat.

The chanting of the crowd was frenzied as they

watched the flames take hold. Emma writhed under the ropes that bound her, but they were too tight for her to wriggle free and she knew that there would be no escape. Desperately, she looked around for some kind of help – anything at all – but her sight was blurred with tears.

And then over the chanting she heard a new noise, a strange *chink, chink, chink*. Her eyes followed the sound to a fresh, blank tombstone that leaned against the side of the courthouse. A man squatted in front of it, his back to the fire. He was tapping against the stone with a chisel, and Emma realized that she already knew what he was going to inscribe: 'Here lie the witch children. 1632.'

The fire was like a living thing now. The dancing flames and billowing smoke were its body, the snap and crackle of the burning wood its voice, and it sang an exultant song in Emma's ears.

And Emma realized that she really could hear a voice. It was a harsh, bitter whisper in her ear, as if a young man was standing right next to her.

'Revenge!' it hissed.

And then another voice chimed in, a girl's voice this time. 'Dance on the grave of witches, would you?' she demanded.

And, with that, Emma understood that *they* had come to watch. The four original witch children, whose grave Abby had danced upon – they were here now, exacting their revenge.

She remembered feeling sorry for the witch children. *Wasted sympathy!* Emma thought. *They really were monsters!*

She opened her mouth and screamed.

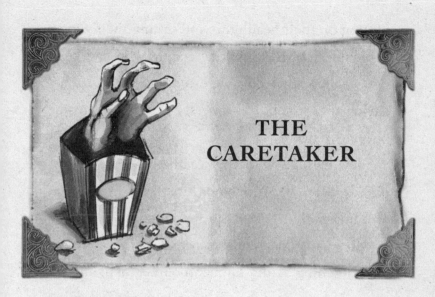

THE
CARETAKER

The wind and the rain arrived together and rattled like steel pellets at the kitchen window. Alex had been reaching up to open a cupboard and he actually flinched at the sudden violence outside. He peered out through the streams of water running down the glass. Trees bent in the wind and curtains of rain gusted along the street. Storm-churned puddles were already forming in the gutters and Alex could see cars slowing down, putting on their headlights and setting their wipers to double speed. An elderly couple who had been out walking their dog were running to find what shelter they could. He was very glad he was inside out of the storm.

'Hey, enough with the weather! We need salt!' called Jason from behind him. His friend was standing at the stove, cooking popcorn.

'More salt!' cried another friend, Ben, staggering and clutching at the kitchen counter, as if his life depended on more salt. 'For the love of God, more salt, that's all we ask!' he howled melodramatically. 'Is there no more salt to be found?'

As Jason and Alex laughed at their friend, the doorbell rang. Alex quickly took the salt from the cupboard. 'Salt,' he said, tossing the container to Ben.

Ben fumbled the catch and dropped the entire container of salt into the pan of popcorn, making Jason crease up with laughter. Alex rolled his eyes and went to answer the front door.

The bell rang again as he hurried into the hall. This time it kept ringing as the visitor kept his finger on the button. Alex undid the latch, and had to brace himself as a sudden gust of damp wind threw the door open for him.

Richard staggered into the house, shaking himself like a dog. 'Flippin' 'eck!' he exclaimed as he undid his coat. 'It's a touch damp out there. Are the others here yet?'

'Yeah.' Alex forced the door closed against the wind. 'They're making a mess in the kitchen – and some popcorn.'

'Popcorn! Cool!' Richard said, throwing his coat over the banisters and following Alex into the kitchen. 'Greetings, loyal fans,' he cried. 'I bless you with my presence. The evening may start now! Thank you, thank you, you are all truly groovy and yes, I'll take that, thanks.'

Ben was holding the bowl of salted popcorn. Richard grabbed it and hotfooted it into the living-room for the best seat.

'Help! Thief! He's got my popcorn!' Ben wailed.

'Little did the popcorn thief know that he had unleashed a mighty force of vengeance that would make him pay dearly!' Jason thundered.

Both boys ran after Richard, leaving Alex to get the drinks from the fridge and follow in his own time.

He paused at the foot of the stairs and called up. 'Mum! Dad! We're starting now. Don't forget that you promised not to disturb us!'

The friends had scheduled this gathering to coincide with his parents' bridge night, but bridge had been cancelled at the last minute. Alex's mum and dad had been very good about being banished upstairs for the evening, but he thought it was worth reminding them.

'Thank you, dear, we wouldn't dream of spoiling your fun,' his mother called back.

'Yes, thank you, Alex,' his father added. 'I think we know the rules!'

Alex turned away towards the living-room,

muttering, 'Yeah, yeah, yeah,' under his breath. Outside, a particularly heavy blast of wind struck the front door. An icy draught rattled through the letterbox and whistled down the hall. The chill air made Alex shiver. 'Ooh, spooky!' he murmured to himself, and grinned. It was like a clichéd scene from a bad horror movie, and a bad horror movie was exactly why he and his three friends had chosen to meet up this Friday evening.

He stepped into the living-room. Ben, Jason and Richard were already lined up on the sofa, passing the popcorn between them.

'Speech! Speech!' Ben called, and the others joined in.

Alex drew the curtains against the foul weather outside, sealing in the warmth and light. Then he took the chosen DVD down from the shelf and squared up in front of his friends. It was a tradition that whoever was hosting should do a short, ironic introduction to that night's movie.

'Thank you, thank you, Jason and gentlemen,' he

announced. This got a cheer from the others and a squawk of protest from Jason, who chucked a cushion at him. Alex caught it with his free hand. 'Welcome to the latest meeting of the Really Rubbish Film Club! Tonight's offering, by popular vote, is . . .' he held the DVD case up and twirled it in his fingers '. . . *The Caretaker*! I would say it's a forgotten classic, except that it's not a classic and no one ever bothered remembering it in the first place. It stars absolutely no one you've ever heard of. It came out in the sixties, flopped at the box office and then promptly vanished until someone dragged it out for late-night TV one Saturday evening a few years ago. I was personally scared out of my skin, but that was nothing compared to at least one person in this room who had to sleep with his mum and dad after watching the film that night – and he was twelve!'

'Nah, Rich wasn't more than eleven,' Ben put in.

'Hey!' Richard protested. 'Who said it was me?'

Alex obligingly handed him the cushion so that he could hit Ben with it.

'My mistake. Must have been Jason,' Ben laughed from underneath the cushion.

'In your dreams!' Jason retorted. 'And, excuse me, but I seem to remember hearing that you famously had to leave the room because you'd wet yourself!'

Ben snatched the cushion from Richard so he could attack Jason. 'I didn't wet myself. I just spilled my Coke!' he protested.

'Yeah, whatever. Got any rubber sheets, Alex?'

Alex grinned and knelt down to put the DVD in the machine.

'So where did the DVD come from?' Jason asked.

'It came free with a magazine,' Alex replied, as he straightened up and the start-up logo appeared on the TV screen. 'The reviewer said it had some interesting extra features.'

'Cool! But later,' said Richard.

'Of course!' Alex agreed. He smiled. 'We've got to have the Really Rubbish bit first!'

The sofa was taken, so he turned the lights off and stretched out on his stomach on the rug by the flickering gas fire. He propped his chin on his arms, and watched as the movie began.

First the logo of a long-forgotten studio appeared out of swirling mists, accompanied by violin strings that set your teeth on edge for all the wrong reasons.

'Nice music,' Ben observed sarcastically. 'All those minor chords to make it sound extra spooky.'

'Nah,' said Jason. 'The musicians just can't play.'

'Sounds like they're playing at the bottom of a deep hole,' Richard complained.

'Not deep enough, if you ask me,' Ben remarked.

Alex smiled to himself and let them chatter. He enjoyed watching the films with his friends but he also liked to pay attention. One day he wanted to do film and media studies at university, maybe go into the business himself. He liked watching how films were made, seeing the tricks used to create a fake reality out of the director's mind. So he kept quiet and watched.

The names of the producers appeared. They wobbled slightly, as if someone was holding them in front of the camera. The violins screeched to a groaning climax that made Alex want to stick his fingers in his ears, and the words 'The Caretaker' flashed on to the screen. The words seemed to have been badly scrawled and superimposed over a photograph of a looming Victorian building that looked like it might have been a school.

To remove any doubt, the scene changed to the entrance of the building, with the word 'School' written over it.

'Just, "School"?' Jason asked. 'No more info?'

'Yeah, I mean, what's its name?' Richard put in.

'I don't think the budget could stretch to thinking up names,' Ben said.

The violins deepened in tone to become more menacing. The names of the actors appeared over still shots of the school – its corridors, its classrooms – all taken at odd angles. Despite the age of the building, the film had been set in what was then the present day – some time in the 1960s. It was in colour, but the colours were very washed out. The picture was scratchy and in desperate need of digital restoration.

Finally all the pictures faded except for a pair of eyes, gazing out malevolently at the viewer. Then the scene started moving and the camera pulled back to reveal that the eyes belonged to an old man in dungarees, his body bent by age, his face cruel and hard.

He shuffled along a corridor, pushing his way through a stream of students pouring out of their classrooms. It was breaktime at the school. Most of the students just ignored the old man but a few were following him, imitating his shuffle and jeering. The man stared straight at the camera, ignoring the torments, while his shoulders rose and fell with laboured breathing.

'Ah! Mr Caretaker, I presume,' said Jason.

'Nah, he's the new James Bond,' Richard joked.

'Does he get the girl?' Ben asked.

'Not the way you're thinking,' Jason replied.

'He hates the students,' Alex said quietly. 'Some of them started a fire a few years ago and that's what damaged his lungs.'

On screen, The Caretaker was still staring at the camera, and Alex had to admit it was an effective technique. It really made you feel as if the old man on screen personally hated *you*.

But the next moment, Alex and his friends were hooting with laughter. The camera had cut to a pair of 'boys' who were scowling at The Caretaker as he shuffled by. They were both at least ten years too old to be playing school pupils and their clothes were absurd concoctions of frills and flares.

'Yay, the sixties!' Jason whooped. 'Taste-free zone!'

'I say, Father,' Ben bleated in an upper-class accent, 'I rather think I will be hip and groovy today.'

'He's pathetic,' said one of the boys on screen, glaring at The Caretaker.

Alex laughed. Ben had got the accent spot on.

'He's pathetic, but he's harmless,' said the second boy dismissively.

'First victim!' Alex, Ben, Richard and Jason chorused. And, sure enough, five minutes later, a teacher sent the second speaker down to a store cupboard to fetch a new box of chalk.

'Chalk? What was this? The Stone Age?' Richard exclaimed.

'Maybe his kids will grow up to invent the interactive whiteboard,' said Ben.

'I don't think he's going to have any kids,' Alex put in.

The boy was now alone in the store cupboard, which looked like the inside of a wobbly cardboard box with a few shelves thrown in for good measure. Alex vaguely remembered this bit from the first time round, but even if he hadn't, there wasn't much doubt about what was going to happen. The screeching violins were back, for a start. They grew louder and louder, and just as they reached their crescendo, The Caretaker loomed out of the darkness behind the victim. He grabbed the boy, putting one large hand over his mouth and dragging him off into the dark.

'And the moral of that is: always travel in pairs when a homicidal maniac is out to get you,' Jason said. 'I wonder how many will learn that lesson before the end of the film.'

'Not many,' Ben predicted. He put his mock accent back on. 'I say, let's split up! He's bound to get one of us!'

'No one knows they're in danger yet,' Alex pointed out.

But that didn't last; as the film unfolded and more pupils began to go missing – all of them the ones who had tormented The Caretaker the most – some of the remaining kids began to realize that something was amiss. The heroes of the movie were three boys and three girls who started to work out what was happening. They called an impromptu meeting in the corner of the playground.

'There's something very wrong here,' said the leading boy on screen. Unlike the actors who had played The Caretaker's early victims, he did look roughly the right age to be a schoolboy. Ignore the early Beatles haircut, Alex thought, and it was actually quite easy to identify with him.

Richard shrugged. 'OK, so he's killing off the bullies. Boohoo. I'm so sad!' he said sarcastically.

'Yeah, let's give him a job at our school,' Ben agreed.

'But he won't stop there, will he?' Alex reminded them.

A small, out-of-focus figure shuffled along the far side of the playground, unseen by the heroes. You couldn't see him clearly but the body language made it clear who he was. The figure stopped and turned his head, and the camera zoomed in to show The Caretaker.

Alex still couldn't name the actor, but he was struck by how good the man was. His body language, his expressions, his *every glance* managed to convey a burning malevolence that drove him to kill again and again and again.

Once it was clear to The Caretaker that the heroes were starting to suspect something, they became the next targets.

Alex had to admire the filmmakers' technique. They hadn't set out to create a group of stereotypical characters – the nice one, the dim one, the geeky one, etc. – like you would so often find in a modern film. These characters were very ordinary and seemed very *real*. Alex was finding it easy to relate to them and to imagine himself in their place. So, when the first one of the group went missing, he really felt it.

The first sign of the character's demise was when the remaining heroes found their friend's glasses lying in a corridor.

'No!' Jason blurted, sounding agonized.

Everyone looked at him. 'I mean, um, I really liked that kid,' he said sheepishly.

'It's just a film, Jase,' said Ben, although Alex thought he sounded quite unnerved himself.

'It's not like it's gory or graphic, either,' Richard said, also sounding uneasy. 'He just grabs them and drags them off. Or they just vanish.'

'Exactly . . .' Alex murmured, unable to take his eyes off the screen. This film wasn't the high body-count, special effects splatterfest like you got out of Hollywood – the sort of horror film Richard was used to. It didn't show the victims with spurting blood and popping eyeballs and severed limbs. But it was all the more scary because of that. And it was affecting all of them.

Alex realized that the filmmakers were deliberately making the viewer see from the survivors' point of view – and all the survivors knew was that their friends were disappearing. They didn't know how and they didn't know why, but they could see that something bad was happening, and, bit by bit, the idea was growing in their own heads: would they be next?

The viewer was encouraged to put him or herself in their place. It was extremely effective and extremely disturbing. Even though Adam could see what the filmmakers were trying to do, he was still feeling spooked.

On screen, the heroes were being overtaken by events. Elsewhere in town, two robbers had decided to hold up a bank, and the ensuing shootout with the police meant that everyone in the school had to stay there. The headmaster carelessly instructed The Caretaker: 'Make the place secure!'

The Caretaker smiled for the first time in the film, and proceeded to lock all the doors and windows. 'All secure, sir,' he told the headmaster, with an ironic salute. It was one of the few times he spoke in the movie and his voice was harsh and grating. 'No one can get . . . in.'

The heroes observed that this meant no one could get out either. Unfortunately, there was nothing they could do to persuade the teachers that anything was wrong, especially as The Caretaker had a knack for turning up in the background whenever they were about to try to voice their concerns. A private conversation with any of the teachers was impossible.

'I know,' Richard said, suddenly breaking the silence and making Alex jump.

No one had spoken for some time. They were all much more caught up in the film than they had expected to be.

'Why don't they all try to talk to a different teacher, all at once?' Richard went on. 'The guy can't be in four different places at the s—'

'Shh!' Jason said abruptly, and Richard fell silent. Everyone's eyes were glued to the screen.

Richard's solution didn't occur to the heroes, but one girl did decide to speak to the headmaster.

The scene showed the interior of the headmaster's office. Through the frosted-glass panel in the door, a figure could be seen approaching. Then the door handle turned slowly and the door swung open. Alex realized he was holding his breath. It was the girl who poked her head around the edge of the door and said timidly, 'Sir? Can I speak to you?'

Alex let his breath out in relief. He had expected the shadowy figure to turn out to be The Caretaker. To judge by the sighs of relief coming from the sofa behind him, his friends had had exactly the same thought.

The camera swung round to show the girl entering the office and walking towards the headmaster's desk. A row of filing cabinets stood against one wall. Alex suddenly remembered what came next, and tensed up again. This scene had made a real impression on him the first time he saw the film.

Ben too. 'The cabinets!' he exclaimed suddenly. 'He's waiting for her behind the cabinets!'

The girl walked past the cabinets and the four friends braced themselves.

Nothing happened.

Alex and Ben exchanged puzzled frowns.

'I thought it was . . .' Ben began.

'Maybe it was another kid later on,' Alex suggested.

'I know,' Jason put in. 'He's standing just out of camera shot, and when she turns round he'll be right there!'

'Yeah, maybe,' Ben agreed. 'But I could have sworn . . .' His voice trailed away as he concentrated on the screen, waiting for the girl to turn round.

The girl on screen did finally turn – only to face nothing but empty air. She shrugged to herself and opened the door to leave the office again.

The Caretaker was standing just the other side of the door, though there had been no sign of him through the glass. Alex, Jason, Richard and Ben all shouted with surprise, and Richard jumped so violently that the remaining popcorn flew out of the bowl.

The old man's hand shot out and he grabbed the girl by the throat. The camera closed in on his face. Once again, his eyes seemed to stare straight out of the screen at the audience, in a chilling manner. Then the scene faded to become the dining hall and the surviving heroes.

'God, I wasn't expecting that,' Ben gasped, and no one teased him.

Watching this film, Alex realized, wasn't as much fun as they had all thought it would be. They hadn't really expected to be scared at all – they thought they knew all the plots and twists in advance, and besides, it was all so dated. But in fact, the film was far more frightening than any of them had remembered.

One by one the heroes were picked off, until finally only one was left. He was walking down the main corridor, calling for his friends, confidently at first, but sounding more and more anxious as he began to realize that he was alone.

He stopped abruptly when he heard a very

faint cry: someone had started to call out his name before they were suddenly cut off. Then he realized he was standing next to the door of the basement. Throughout the film, it had often appeared in the background, but it had always been firmly shut with an 'Out of Bounds' notice pinned to it. Now it was ever so slightly ajar.

The last remaining hero of the film pushed the door open a little further and walked in. There was a flight of concrete steps, lit by a single, bare electric light bulb, leading to the basement. The steps disappeared down into the dark, past pipes and ducts and fuse boxes. The boy strained his eyes, trying to see into the darkness, and drew a breath as if to call out 'Hello?'

Alex winced. *No! Don't let him know you're there*, he thought.

As if he could read Alex's mind, the boy let his breath out again without a sound. Then he began to walk slowly down the stairs, making as little noise as possible. Halfway down, his toes nudged a discarded beer can and it scraped the concrete. Everyone tensed, waiting for it to clatter down the stairs. But it teetered on the edge and the boy quickly bent down and scooped it up, setting it down again right out of the way.

At the bottom of the stairs were two doors. One had a sign on it labelled 'Heating', and was firmly padlocked shut. The boy tested the padlock, then turned to the other door. This was smaller, with a grille set into it. It was closed, but there was no padlock. The boy gripped the doorknob and twisted it slowly. He paused for a moment to summon his courage, and then flung the door wide.

There was no light on inside so he had to step into the dark. He fumbled on the wall for a light switch but couldn't find one. He was forced to go further into the room, away from the door, which swung shut behind him with an ominous *thud*. For a brief moment the room was in pitch darkness, but then there was a click and the light came on. The boy stood with one hand on the switch, looking around.

A bare light bulb cast a weak, yellow glow over the room. Shadows danced all round the edges, making it hard to see exactly what was what. The camera showed some cupboards, some school desks and some piles of other junk. But as the boy and the camera scanned the room, what looked like a pile of discarded rubbish bags in one corner resolved into a pile of dead bodies.

The boy forgot his caution and ran forward, falling to his knees in front of the corpses. His face was contorted with horror and tears rolled down his cheeks. The bodies at the top of the pile were the boy's friends, their features twisted and distorted in silent screams.

Behind the boy, on the other side of the room, one of the shadows seemed to come to life. The Caretaker stepped out into the light.

'Seen enough, boy?' he asked.

The boy spun round to face him. 'You killed them!' he gasped.

'Did I?' The Caretaker demanded harshly. '*Did I?* Look closer.'

The boy peered at the bodies and his eyes widened. 'There's not a mark on them,' he murmured in disbelief.

'No,' The Caretaker agreed, closing in on the boy with a vindictive grin on his face, while the boy himself seemed rooted to the spot. 'I'm not a pathetic little bully like these,' The Caretaker spat, gesturing to the pile of bodies. 'I use a weapon they would never understand. Know what that is, boy?'

The boy mutely shook his head.

'The mind! I get into their minds, that's what I do. I scare them senseless. I drag out their deepest, darkest fears and make them real. I am their worst nightmare – and they *can't wake up*. They can only die!' The Caretaker said with satisfaction.

And then he turned to the camera and Alex felt as if the insane old man was staring right into his eyes. 'After all,' The Caretaker added, 'best to die screaming, don't you think?'

And with that he moved off camera, leaving the picture fixed on the pile of bodies. The violins screeched to a final climax and the words 'THE END' appeared in the middle of the television screen.

Alex made a grab for the remote control and pointed it at the TV. The DVD whirred and froze, and then the picture blanked as the disc ejected smoothly from the machine.

'Hey, what about the special features?' Jason protested. 'Ow!' he added, momentarily blinded as Richard jumped up and switched on the light.

The boys blinked at each other, no one quite sure what to say.

'That was . . . different,' Ben said.

'Yeah. It was, uh, well, you know – the atmosphere got to you after a while,' Alex offered.

'Hah! Yeah,' Richard said, but his attempt at a laugh was a little too sharp.

'So, no special features, then,' Jason grumbled, but Alex could see relief in his eyes.

Conversation lapsed again. Alex knew that according to tradition, the host should deliver a closing speech to sum up the film they had just seen, but he really didn't want to. He was angry that he felt so shaken. He reminded himself that he was warm and safe in his own home, with the lights on and the fire burning. Gradually, he started to feel the chill of the film slip away.

He was just about to make an attempt at a closing speech when a car horn hooted outside. All four boys jumped.

'That'll be my dad,' Jason said, and there was a mini-stampede for the door. Jason's dad had agreed to take all three of Alex's visitors home.

'I guess you'll be off, then,' Alex said reluctantly. He felt like he could do with some company for a little while longer. But the others were already putting their coats on. Alex squared his shoulders and followed them into the hall.

Ben opened the front door and a blast of cold air blew into their faces.

'OK, so, same time next week?' Alex said hopefully.

'Sure. At Ben's place,' Jason replied. 'Hey, Ben, get a comedy or something, right?'

'No problem,' Ben agreed enthusiastically.

And in another moment they were gone, running out through the dark and the rain to the car. Alex stood in the door with his hands in his pockets and watched them leave. *At least I don't have to run through that*, he thought, determined to be optimistic about something. The car doors slammed and his friends waved as the car pulled away.

Alex shut the door and double-locked it. He turned away, paused, and turned back to give the door an extra tug. Just checking. He paused again, then put the chain on.

'Grow up, grow up, grow up!' he muttered

angrily to himself as he walked down the hall towards the kitchen and the back door. Without his friends the house seemed eerily quiet. Alex couldn't hear any noise from the TV in his parents' room and there didn't seem to be any lights on upstairs.

The stairs started in brightness downstairs where the lights were on, then disappeared into blackness at the top where they met the upstairs landing. Just like the stairs to the basement in *The Caretaker*, Alex thought, only they went down instead of up. Then he told himself sharply to stop thinking about the film.

Alex got to the kitchen and stopped. Across it he could see his own reflection in the glass of the back door, his body silhouetted in a rectangle of light. He could easily get across the kitchen in the dark, but somehow he didn't want to watch his reflection walking towards him. He flicked the switch and the neon tube on the ceiling started to flicker. It always took ages to warm up and come on properly. Alex grimaced and walked towards the back door, his reflection appearing and disappearing with the light. He locked the back door and returned to the hall, just in time for the light to come on and stay on. He glowered at it, turned it off again and shut the kitchen door behind him.

I get into their minds – that's what The Caretaker had said. Well, Alex thought, the old man had certainly managed to get into his! He squinted up the stairs again. There was still no sound or light. His parents must have gone to bed. And that, he decided, was what he would do himself. Being the only one up and about was really creeping him out. He figured he would turn in, maybe read a few chapters of something light and funny, and go to sleep. Tomorrow he would meet up with the guys again and they could all have a good laugh about the film.

Alex went into the living-room to tidy up and turn the TV off. But as he stepped into the room, the

DVD whirred and the tray holding the disc slid back into the machine.

'What the . . .?' Alex murmured. He looked down at his feet to see if he had stepped on the remote control by mistake. But no, it was where he had left it, on the hearth rug.

For the second time that evening the studio logo appeared from the mists as the film began to play on screen. The violins cut in, and Alex lunged for the remote control and hit the 'mute' button. He didn't need to listen to creepy violin music right now, he was feeling edgy enough as it was. But the remote control had no effect.

He wandered closer to the TV and hit the button again. A high-pitched whistle began to sound at the very edges of his hearing and Alex grimaced. It was like the sound of a dentist's drill drifting down a very long corridor, just annoying enough to make his ears ache. He jabbed the 'stop' button on the remote, but still nothing happened. The credits continued to roll.

'Come on . . .' he murmured irritably, trying again. It didn't work. Alex figured that the batteries must have gone flat. Still the credits were rolling, now at the stage where they showed the school from different angles.

Alex felt his film-buff eye taking over. Although he really wanted to just shut the TV off and go to bed – if only to get rid of that irritating whistle – a bigger part of him was being drawn into the film again. He hadn't realized it the first time round, but the credits were showing the settings where, later on, each of The Caretaker's victims fell into his hands. It was a clever bit of prefiguring. Abruptly, all the fears which the first screening had stirred up in Alex came rushing back more strongly than ever.

'OK, that's enough!' he snapped aloud. Since the remote control wasn't working, he knelt down and pressed 'eject' on the machine itself. But the DVD obstinately kept playing. Alex sighed and jammed his finger against the 'eject' button. He held it there, willing the machine to take notice. It continued to ignore him.

The credits faded and the first scene appeared. Alex remembered that it was the scene where The Caretaker slouched down the corridor, his face set against the taunts and the insults thrown at him. But Alex blinked and looked twice because, this time, there was no caretaker!

Alex had never seen a DVD go wrong like this before. The screen showed the same group of cruel teenagers and, in the middle of them, an empty space. It was as if the pixels had been stripped out of the image. The shape was man-shaped and it moved like a man walking, or rather limping, along in The Caretaker's recognizable style. But The Caretaker was not there. The shape was simply filled in with the static you get on a broken TV screen, and it fizzed in time with the screeching sound that was still ringing subtly in Alex's ears.

'Weird!' Alex murmured. He pulled down the DVD box and scanned the text quickly. Was it one of those special features they had never got round to exploring? Had the DVD producers used some CGI to play about with the original movie? But what was the point? Alex wondered. It was a pretty unusual special feature – if it was one.

Oh, God, Alex thought. *I really don't need this*. It was too weird and he didn't want weird, he wanted normality. He hit the 'eject' button even more urgently, still with no effect. Then his eyes fell on the plugs in the wall. Hurriedly, he moved over and pulled all the plugs from the sockets.

The TV and DVD displays went dead. The movie vanished into a dark screen. Alex knelt with the plugs dangling from his hand and heaved a sigh of relief. His dad would have had a fit if he'd known. Alex could already hear his father's voice in his head: *You have to shut it down properly! Properly! Do you want it to break? Do you think I'm made of money?* But Alex was just relieved that the movie had stopped.

He caught a flicker of movement out of the

corner of his eye and he spun round. 'Dad?' he called, feeling a pang of guilt. His dad sometimes came down to double-check the locks. Alex didn't relish the thought of being found with the plugs in his hand. Especially since his explanation would sound so lame: 'I was really spooked by the scary film . . .'

Alex got to his feet and walked out into the hallway to see what had caught his eye. The doors to the kitchen and the dining-room were shut, and there was nothing and nobody in the hall. If somebody was downstairs they could only be in one of those two other rooms. Alex knew that the kitchen door creaked, and he would have heard it if it had opened, so he could tick that one off. He glared at the dining-room door, thinking of the boy in the film and the door down in the basement. Then he bit his lip, pushed the dining-room door open and reached in to turn the light on.

Apart from the usual dining-table, chairs and sideboard, the room was completely empty.

Alex backed into the hall again, pulling the door shut behind him. There was only upstairs left, unless he had imagined the movement – which he might well have done in his current nervous state. Just then, a *thud* sounded on the landing above. Alex glanced up at the ceiling. Cautiously, he walked to the foot of the stairs and peered up into the darkness.

'Are you there, Dad?' he called. There was no answer, but he knew he had heard something up there. It was a modern house and the floorboards didn't creak. They didn't have a cat. And if it was his parents, surely they would turn a light on. Unless . . .

Unless it's just a wind-up! Alex thought. He remembered his mum asking what the boys were going to be watching that night. He had happily told her all about the film. So, both his parents could have known about it. And sometimes his dad did like to play jokes on him. But if this was just a wind-up then it was so not funny.

His eyes were fixed on the dark landing at the top of the stairs. Which was more likely? Alex asked himself. That his dad was playing some kind of game, or that there was an intruder in the house? They both seemed equally improbable to Alex, but there was only one way to find out. He decided to go upstairs and see.

He made his way up the first few stairs and once again found his mind drifting back to the stairs that led to the basement in *The Caretaker*. He tried to reassure himself with the thought that, whatever he found, it wouldn't be the dead bodies of Jason and Richard and Ben. He had seen them leave.

It suddenly struck him that his friends couldn't have got far. He felt for his mobile in his back pocket. He could ask them to come back and help. Then he shook his head and took his hand away. If there wasn't an intruder – and there probably wasn't – then they would think he was mad. Plus they would take the mickey out of him for the rest of his life!

He began to make his way, very slowly, up the rest of the stairs.

Alex knew the way well enough to do it by feel, so he didn't turn the landing light on. He knew he was acting like a typical teenager in a film like *The Caretaker*, but he didn't want anyone to know he was coming – whether there *was* an intruder upstairs or whether it was just his dad winding him up.

When his head became level with the landing, he peered around cautiously. He could see reasonably well, thanks to a sliver of moonlight streaming in through the landing curtains. There was nothing but the dark square of the bookcase and the even darker outlines of the doors: the bathroom, his own room, the spare room and his parents' room. All the doors were ajar to varying degrees.

Except that his parents' door chose that exact moment to slam shut, almost as if someone had been waiting for him to get up there.

Alex jumped and had to clutch the banister to

keep his balance. Anger flooded through him. 'All right, this isn't funny!' he snapped aloud.

He crossed the landing in two strides – annoyance overriding his unease – and reached out to grab the door handle. But as his fingers closed around the doorknob, he felt something warm and wet and slimy. Quickly, he pulled his hand away and looked down at his open palm. The moonlight reduced everything to silvery shades of grey, but he could see that there was something dark and wet on his skin.

The little knot of fear in Alex's stomach, which had been there ever since he saw that sudden movement out of the corner of his eye downstairs, suddenly threatened to overwhelm him. He wanted to turn and flee, out of the house, into the rain, not stopping until he had reached Richard's house, his nearest friend. But his legs felt like they had turned to jelly and, besides, it was his parents who were on the other side of that door. He needed to know what was going on.

Slowly, gradually, Alex made himself look up at the door in front of him. His heart was pounding so loudly he thought it could probably be heard downstairs, and yet, despite that, he thought he could hear something else too. He cocked his head to bring one ear closer to the door.

And there was a sound, he was sure of it. It was the faintest whisper, the slightest suggestion of a harsh rasping noise, regular and repeated – and horribly like the breathing of The Caretaker from the movie.

A sudden burst of anger gave Alex the strength to move. He was determined not to let himself be freaked out by a character from a film. 'Right, joke's over!' he said loudly, and pushed the door open.

He stood in the doorway, apprehensively looking around. The familiar warm smell of his parents' room filled his nostrils, which was comforting. But there was no moonlight spilling through the curtains here, nothing to penetrate the darkness and show him anything of what was inside the room. Alex took a brave step forward.

Once he had properly entered the room he could see the outline of his parents' bed, and the shapes of their bodies beneath the quilt. But where the quilt was a plain, pale yellow in daylight, now he could see an ugly dark stain spread all over it. His mother's hand, pale and limp, hung down the side of the bed.

Alex's mouth moved, but his voice had dried to nothing and he had to try again. 'Mum? Dad? *Mum?*' he called fearfully.

He could sense the truth – it was already somewhere at the back of his mind – but he didn't want to face it. He *couldn't* face it. Hoping against hope, he walked slowly over to the bed.

Abruptly, the door slammed shut behind him. Alex froze. Now there was no doubt about it – he could hear breathing. It was only a few feet away and it wasn't coming from his parents' bed. There was only one way to find out whose breathing it was.

While every particle of his being screamed at him to run, Alex forced himself to turn round. And then he saw that – in any case – there was nowhere to run. The only way out was through the door, and a hunched figure now stood in front of it, seemingly peering intently at Alex.

As Alex stared, the figure limped forward and The Caretaker emerged from the shadows. Alex recognized the familiar twisted grin on his face and saw a glint in his eye.

'They didn't die screaming,' The Caretaker said in his hideous, cracked voice.

Alex nodded a silent, dazed acknowledgement. It was the only movement he could make. His whole reason shrieked outrage. The Caretaker was a character in a film, played by a long-forgotten actor. And yet here he stood! Alex's brain reeled with the impossibility of the situation, as the terror welled up inside him.

'I couldn't get into their heads,' the old man continued. 'They were too tough for me.

They'd grown up, seen it all, you see. Couldn't be frightened. But you?' The Caretaker chuckled and took a step forwards. 'Now, you're a different matter . . .'

FINDERS KEEPERS

Joe Wright had all his attention on the soccer game, so he didn't see Kate Morrison come into the park. But he did catch a brief glimpse of her out of the corner of his eye, as he sprinted past while she stood on the touchlines. He noticed her because of the colour of her hair, somewhere between blonde and auburn, and the angle of her head, the way she always seemed to be looking up at you slightly, as if sizing you up and liking what she saw. Yes! It was Kate, all right.

Joe saw that Kate was surrounded by a group of friends — stuck-up Donna Covington and all the usual faces. At the same time he spotted the gap in the other team's defence. Perfect!

It was the usual, informal Sunday afternoon game. Joe's team had possession of the ball — it was with one of his friends, Simon — but three boys from the other team were closing in. The turf flashed by beneath his feet as Joe ran parallel to Simon, shouting, 'To me! To me!'

There was a wide open stretch of pitch ahead. Simon heard and glanced over at Joe, took in the approaching defenders, and then passed the ball with a cross that sent it flying through the air.

It overshot a bit and Joe jumped to catch it on his chest. He hit the ground and kept running, neatly bringing the ball under control with his feet. He had to swerve suddenly as another defender came at him, but this brought him into direct line with the goal. Unfortunately, the other team were getting their act together now. The goalie had seen him coming and the other defenders were making a wall between Joe and the net. Joe looked around, but there was no one to pass to. And Kate Morrison was watching . . .

Joe drew back his foot and kicked the ball hard, giving it just the right amount of spin to send it curving through the air above the defenders and into the net.

'GOAL!' Joe yelled in delight as his team celebrated, and Simon ran over with a broad grin on his face to give him a high five.

Joe looked over at Kate, the only one whose opinion really mattered to him. His grin faded when he realized that she was no longer watching, and probably hadn't seen any of what had just happened. There was the rattle of wheels on concrete and a posse of skateboarders rolled past, laughing and chatting, with Lee Hartigan in the lead. Every head, Kate's included, had turned to follow them.

'Oh, great!' Joe muttered. His shoulders sagged. 'Cheers, Lee.'

Lee was heading straight for the curved ramp at the corner of the park. Accompanied by two of his buddies he flew up into the air. Time seemed to slow as he hung suspended, revolving slowly, his board somehow staying at his feet.

How does he do that? Joe wondered in frustration.

Then things picked up again and the gang came flashing back down to earth. Their legs flexed as their wheels hit the ground and then they were cruising back the way they had come.

Kate and her friends applauded.

'I could do that,' Joe muttered, but only to himself. The few times he had been on a skateboard he had been reasonably good. At least, he hadn't fallen off. Unfortunately, not owning a skateboard made it kind of hard to practise and get any better. Joe wished he could get one, but there wasn't much money for luxuries like skateboards in Joe's house, or games, or designer clothes, or latest-generation mobile phones – all the things that Lee and his friends seemed to take for granted.

'Hey, Joe!' Simon called. He was holding the ball and spinning it between his hands. 'Want to kick us off again?'

Somehow Joe's heart wasn't in the game any more. 'Nah,' he called back. 'You take over.'

Simon looked a bit disappointed, but he shrugged and tossed the ball to someone else as Joe slouched off the pitch. Joe really didn't want to hang around while Lee did some other flash skateboarding trick to show how cool he was. Unfortunately, to leave the park he had to walk past the skateboard ramps.

Lee's two companions had peeled off and slowed down, but Lee was heading for the other ramp and Joe heard him shout: 'Going for a five-forty!'

Lee's wheels hit the ramp and again he and his board were flung up into the sky. Joe found he had paused, watching and holding his breath along with everyone else. Lee turned . . . One hundred and eighty degrees – he was facing back the way he had come. Three hundred and sixty – he was facing away again. And then, just as gravity seemed to notice he was missing and start to draw him back to earth, he managed another one hundred and eighty. A full circle and a half, 540 degrees, as he plummeted back to the ground again.

The park erupted in applause and a grinning Lee coasted to a stop with his arms held high, acknowledging the cheers.

'Here I come, Tony Hawk!' he shouted. He gave one last kick-stamp and his board flew up into his hands. Then, as if Joe didn't feel sick enough already, he headed over towards Kate and her friends. Feeling cross with himself for having stopped to watch, Joe started walking again.

'Joe! Hi!'

Joe's heart skipped a beat as he turned towards the voice.

Kate was waving cheerfully over at him. 'Hey!' she called again. 'Want to come over?'

'I, uh . . .' Joe took a step in her direction, but beyond Kate he could see Lee, who didn't look very pleased at Kate's invitation. His gaze was neutral but Joe thought he could see a certain steel in the other boy's eyes. And Lee was twirling his board in his hands, like Joe just had to take another step and Lee would be on it again, impressing the heck out of everyone in a way Joe never could.

'Uh, thanks, but I have to . . .' Joe cast about hopelessly for an excuse that wouldn't sound too lame. 'Uh, homework,' he said, managing to find the lamest excuse of all.

'Homework?' Kate sounded sceptical. 'OK. Have fun.'

'Yeah, uh, you too . . .' Joe turned away, his face burning. Walking out of the park took about thirty seconds, but it seemed to take for ever and he had to fight the temptation to bang his head against every lamppost he passed.

Clang!

The pebble Joe had kicked clattered against the metal shutter outside the shop. Joe wandered home along Summer Hill, leaving the park and Kate Morrison and Lee Hartigan safely behind. During the week, even in the evenings, Summer Hill was the heart of the town – a long, straight road lined with shops, cafés and restaurants – where Joe would sometimes hang out with his friends.

However, on a Sunday almost everywhere was closed, and Summer Hill was a lonely and desolate concrete drive. The wind gusted down the road, carrying dead leaves and litter from the park. The blank, metal shutters of the shops were cold and unfriendly, as if the stores had turned their backs on the town and were denying it the light and life they brought at other times. They offered hope and promise, but, right now, they wouldn't deliver. Somehow that fitted Joe's mood exactly.

He kicked another stone. *Clang!* It was a grating, metallic noise – the kind of noise that would be guaranteed to annoy anyone. That also fitted Joe's mood. It was satisfying, almost therapeutic.

He wandered past one of the few open establishments – a new pizza shop that had just started business. The smell of baking drifted into the street and made his stomach growl. But Joe couldn't go in there for the same reason he couldn't practise his skateboarding skills. It all came down to money, and the fact that he didn't have any.

'Life's not all about money,' his father had said a few days ago.

Yeah, right! Joe thought.

His dad had also said, 'You're a nice kid, Joe, and if a girl's nice too then she won't care about money.'

Joe thought about this and had to admit that his dad was probably right. Kate Morrison didn't hang around with Lee because the other boy was rich. She was better than that. She hung around with him because he could make her laugh – and he showed an interest in her and he didn't fob her off with lame excuses about homework!

No, it wasn't just the money. But Joe couldn't shake the feeling that the money probably helped.

Thud!

Joe had taken a step further before he realized the last pebble had hit something soft. He glanced down in irritation. He wanted another good, satisfying *clang!*

A layer of rubbish had accumulated along the side of the pavement, blown up against the foot of the shutters. The pebble had bounced off something small and black, and it took Joe a moment to see that it was a wallet, lying discarded amongst all the debris. It lay against one of the shutters, like it had been kicked there by someone without them realizing. He stooped to pick it up, then glanced about to see if the owner was anywhere nearby.

There was an old lady walking her dog on the other side of the road. Further along, a group of younger boys were kicking a football against a wall. But they were the only signs of life, and

Joe realized immediately that none of them was the owner. The lady would have had a purse, not a wallet, and the kids were too young. He took a final look around. No, there was no one else in sight.

He turned the wallet over in his hands. It was made of battered black leather, scuffed and well worn. It felt quite thick. Maybe there would be something inside with the owner's address on it. He opened the wallet up, and a wad of bank-notes, a centimetre thick, unfolded in front of him.

'Wow!' Joe exclaimed. He flicked through the wad quickly. Most of the notes seemed to be fifties and twenties. He didn't think he had ever even *seen* a fifty-pound note before, but he could count them pretty quickly. He was holding close to a thousand pounds in his hand.

Whoever owned the wallet was definitely going to want it back. He rummaged quickly through the other compartments. There wasn't a driving licence or anything to say where the owner lived. There was no picture ID either. But there was a credit card with a name on it: Mr Mitchell Murray.

Joe knew he had to tell someone about this. He debated which was nearer – home or the police station. He figured it was about the same distance to both of them, so he decided he would drop the wallet off at the police station – though he had to admit, as he looked down at the money, that it would be a shame to see the last of all that cash. However, since Mr Mitchell Murray was obviously rolling in money, Joe hoped there would be a decent reward. He tucked the wallet into the inside pocket of his coat and set off.

Five minutes later he was at the T-junction at the end of Summer Hill, where he had to turn left for the police station or right for home. He started left, then paused. He thought about going home and calling the police from there. Then they could come to him. Pleased with that idea, he headed off in that direction, but again he paused. The wallet wasn't his and maybe Mr Mitchell Murray was frantic with worry right now. Joe decided he should go to the police station straight away and get it over with. He turned back again . . .

This time the games shop on the other side of the road caught his eye. He knew it well – the manager could be a pain, but one of the assistants was friendly and always let Joe play on the demos without actually buying anything.

There was a new poster in the shop window. Joe crossed the road for a closer look and found himself staring straight down the barrel of a massive pistol, wielded by a robot studded with lethal killing devices. Above it the blocky, metallic letters spelled out: 'TECH ASSASSIN'.

'Hey, they got it at last!' he murmured. The magazines had been full of advance previews of the game for months, and it sounded really cool. Joe stepped back to admire the display. Through the window, towards the back of the shop, he could see a display stand overflowing with copies.

And then it hit him. Suddenly it wasn't a

thousand pounds he had on him any more, it was *opportunity*. All the things Joe couldn't do before because he didn't have the money, he now could – for as long as the money lasted anyway. He looked up at the poster again. 'You know what they say,' he said to himself longingly. 'Finders keepers!'

No! he thought firmly. *No way!* He wasn't going to start spending a stranger's money, just like that. But that was only what his conscience told him. The rest of him was feeling very tempted . . .

Joe sat down on a bench, pulled the wallet out of his pocket and looked at it thoughtfully. It wasn't his money. He knew he shouldn't spend it, but somehow he couldn't quite bring himself to part with it either.

He was still sitting there ten minutes later when he heard Kate Morrison's voice again.

'Hi, Joe!'

He looked up. Kate was standing on the other side of the road, smiling. The sun was getting low in the sky and it gave her red-gold hair a golden glow that shone around her head. That, and the smile, made Joe's heart skip a beat. He felt his pulse quicken as he quickly checked the street for traffic – which also let him see that, yes, Kate was on her own – and then hurried over to join her.

'Hi,' he said, vaguely aware that he was grinning like an idiot. He tried to look cool instead. 'So, what brings you here?'

'I live this way,' she said, pointing further down the road.

'Oh. Yeah. Uh, me too.' Joe bit his tongue. He wanted to seem cool but he really wasn't sounding it.

'So . . . did you get your homework done?' Kate asked, with a smile and a sideways look at him.

Joe cursed the stupid, stupid excuse he had made earlier. 'Um . . . no,' he said. He had been about to say yes, but common sense told him she would know he hadn't had the time. He couldn't have gone home, done his homework and got back here since he last saw her. 'I, uh, remembered it's not due in till Thursday,' he explained. 'So, uh, you want to walk?'

'Sure. That'd be nice.'

They started walking together down the road.

'I was going to get a snack but I left my purse at home,' Kate said. 'I'm starving.'

'Yeah, me too . . .' Joe stopped abruptly. He remembered the pizza place back on Summer Hill, and the delicious, warm smell of baking dough.

And he had the money to treat Kate now.

But it wasn't *his* money, he thought. Although, there was bound to be a reward when he handed it in, wasn't there? He wondered how much it would be. Well, Mr Mitchell Murray was obviously a wealthy man, so Joe figured he'd probably get at least a fifty-pound note by way of thanks. In fact, he could really just slip a fifty out now, as a kind of reward in advance, couldn't he?

But then, Joe realized, if Mr Mitchell Murray did come forward to claim the wallet, he would know that there was money missing. In which case, wouldn't it be better not to hand the wallet in at all?

What it came down to, right then and there in Joe's head, was who did he care about more: some stranger or Kate Morrison? And put that way, it was a no-brainer.

'Do you want a pizza?' he asked, his heart racing again. 'My treat.'

He could tell he had surprised Kate, but it must have been in a good way because she smiled at him. 'Yeah, thanks,' she said. 'That would be really good.'

'This is great,' Kate said, twenty minutes later, as the waitress set their orders in front of them. Chicken and pineapple for her, ham and mushroom for him, and a garlic bread to share. 'The pizza smells delicious!'

'Yeah,' Joe agreed, sniffing his pizza appreciatively.

Kate looked around and Joe followed her gaze. The place was decorated with terracotta paint and tiles, in what he supposed was a genuine Italian style.

Kate turned back to Joe. 'It's really nice,' she said.

'Yes, I think they just finished decorating,' Joe told her.

'I meant, being here with you,' she said, smiling shyly.

Joe felt his cheeks burn. 'Yeah. And, uh, you too,' he replied awkwardly. *Oh, for God's sake,* a voice inside him screamed, *learn to say something interesting!*

'I saw that goal you scored earlier,' she said. 'That was cool.'

'You saw that? Really?' he asked, surprised. 'I thought you were looking at . . .' He paused, thinking that he didn't want to bring Lee's name into the conversation. 'I thought you were looking at something else,' he finished instead.

'Well, I don't know if you saw, but Lee came along and he does make a lot of noise,' Kate laughed. 'But I saw the goal. Good one.'

She took a bite out of her pizza while Joe's heart sang. *She had seen his goal!* That was so great. Now he just had to build on that by finding the right things to say . . .

'Do you eat out often?' Kate asked. 'I don't, but then my dad won't let me get a job. I expect you've got a paper round or something?'

'Yes, yes I have,' Joe said honestly. He *did* have a paper round. It just didn't pay quite as well as Mr Mitchell Murray. He felt a stab of guilt at the thought, but he pushed it away. He was sticking to his earlier reasoning – the pizza money would be his reward from the wallet's grateful owner.

'But I don't eat out often,' Joe went on, also quite truthfully. 'Only for special occasions.'

And from the way Kate smiled back at him, he guessed he had finally found the right thing to say.

Joe finally got home at ten that night, an hour later than he had said he'd be back.

'You've been *where?*' his mum demanded when he told his parents. 'Eating *pizza?*'

'Not much point sending him to bed without any

dinner, then,' his dad said, giving Joe a wink. 'Who's the girl?'

'That's not the point . . .' his mum insisted. Joe carefully kept his eyes on the floor, trying to look sorry and not too pleased with himself.

Eventually his mum pinched his cheek. 'OK, you're old enough to stay out a bit, but for goodness' sake let us know first. Now get upstairs to bed. It's school tomorrow, remember?'

So Joe went up for a shower and bed, grinning to himself because he'd had a whole evening of Kate's undivided attention, and it felt great.

He wondered if she was officially his girlfriend now. That would be cool. He'd turn up at school tomorrow morning, saunter up to her and say casually, 'Hi, Kate.' And she would smile at him and say 'Hi' back.

And if Lee Hartigan was somewhere in the vicinity, well, that would just be the icing on the cake.

The last thing Joe did, before turning the light

out, was place Mr Mitchell Murray's bulging wallet carefully under his pillow. It seemed like the most normal thing in the world.

Joe went to school the next day walking on air. In fact, he was in such a good mood that on the way he popped into the newsagent's to buy a massive bar of nut and toffee chocolate.

One of the things he and Kate had talked about had been favourite foods.

'One of those big bars, you know, with the toffee and nuts in. Mmmm,' she had said dreamily. So Joe had made a mental note that the next day, that was what she would get. He would give it to her at registration. Normally it would have made quite a dent in his allowance. This time he didn't even notice the cost.

When he reached school, a quick look around the playground soon showed that Kate wasn't about. Maybe she was inside. Joe bounded up the steps to the front doors two at a time, just as Lee

Hartigan started coming down in the other direction. Oh, this was too good! For the first time ever, Joe felt confident enough to look Lee in the eye and say, 'Hi, Lee.'

Lee looked at him sourly without breaking his step. 'Don't know what you're so pleased about,' he said and carried on.

Joe shrugged. *OK, sore loser!* he thought.

A small knot of girls at the top of the steps chose that moment to start giggling. He glanced at them. Were they laughing because Lee had given him the brush-off? Or just because girls liked to giggle? Joe wasn't sure, but who cared? He and Kate were practically an item!

Joe pushed through the swing doors. Kate wasn't in the lobby, either, but there was another cluster of girls over by the notice-board. This time he could swear one of them saw him and nudged her friend, before they all looked over at him and then burst into stifled giggles.

'OK,' he muttered, frowning. One bout of

laughter at his appearance he could live with, but two was getting annoying.

He turned away and saw Donna Covington coming down the corridor. Donna was with the usual bunch of friends that hung out with Kate, but Kate wasn't with them.

Normally Joe wouldn't even try to speak to Donna; she was never friendly. But today, buoyed up with courage from the previous evening, he approached her. 'Hi, Donna,' he said casually, like they were really close acquaintances. 'Do you know where Kate is?'

The entire group burst into sniggers and even Donna's look of disdain flickered slightly with a smile.

'She's at home, in bed,' she said.

'Oh.' Joe hadn't expected that at all, and he had no idea what to say. 'Um. Is she ill? Got a cold?'

Donna grinned, like a shark baring its teeth. 'Her mum says it's food poisoning,' she said with relish.

'Kate was throwing up all night. Seems some jerk gave her bad pizza.'

Joe gaped in horror.

'Here's a free tip, Wright,' Donna whispered maliciously, as the others moved off. 'Girls generally prefer it if you don't try to poison them on the first date.'

It got worse. By lunch-time, it felt like everyone in the school had heard about Kate's food poisoning. Some couldn't hide their cold amusement, others were good enough to look sorry for Joe, but Joe didn't want pity. He just wanted Kate to be healthy and well again.

It wasn't so bad during the lessons because at least then he could concentrate on work, but when lunch came, his friends were sitting with Lee's crowd and he couldn't face the thought of joining them. So he took his sandwiches out on to the playing fields and munched them on his own.

As he pushed his lunch box back into his bag,

Joe's fingers brushed against the chocolate bar he had bought for Kate. He pulled it out and glared at it as if it had caused all his problems. It should have been something that would make Kate smile, but, under the circumstances, the bright, shiny wrapper just seemed to mock him.

Well, Kate wouldn't be wanting the chocolate any day soon, Joe thought – if she ever wanted to see him again at all. So he tore back a strip of paper and broke off the first row of chocolate chunks.

He bit into it eagerly, but soon decided that it was far too sweet, in a way that made his teeth ache. He drew back his hand to chuck the remaining chunks of chocolate into the bushes, but then he stopped. 'Money isn't to be wasted,' his dad always said. And old habits died hard. Joe had always been brought up to finish every meal. So he made himself finish the row of chocolate.

He put the final piece into his mouth and bit into it. *Crack!* A white-hot needle of pain shot through his jaw, and Joe would have cried out if his mouth hadn't been full of chocolate. Instead he went 'Mmph!' and clutched his face in pain.

Eventually, he swallowed the chocolate and the pain subsided. Tentatively Joe explored the inside of his mouth with his tongue. He moved it slowly back over his molars until he felt an unfamiliar rough shape at the back of his mouth and got another explosion of pain.

Oh, great! Joe thought. He had cracked a tooth on a bar of chocolate! How had that happened? This was definitely not his lucky day.

By the end of the day, Joe was very happy to leave school. On top of his humiliation over Kate's food poisoning and then his pain from the broken tooth, he had had to phone his mum and ask her to fix up a dentist's appointment for him. Of course, that meant answering a hundred anxious questions about how he'd broken the tooth in the first place and whether it was still painful and so on and so on.

Now he slouched moodily along Summer Hill and glared with dislike at the line of shops. This was where it had all started, he thought bitterly. If he hadn't found that wallet then he wouldn't have bought the pizza, or the chocolate, and Kate would be healthy, no one would have poked fun at him in school, and his mouth wouldn't be in pain.

The street was more alive than it had been twenty-four hours previously. The shutters were up and the shops were still open. Joe's usual route took him up to the junction at the end of Summer Hill, and there, right opposite Joe, was the games shop. The *Tech Assassin* poster was still up in the window, bright and alluring.

Joe put his hand into his pocket to feel the wallet. His fingertips brushed against the leather as he thought things over. Fact: the money still wasn't his. Fact: he still felt he deserved some kind of reward for handing the wallet in – which, admittedly, he hadn't done yet, but he still intended to. And fact: so far the money hadn't been any reward at all. His would-be girlfriend was ill in bed and he'd broken a tooth. It was about time the money brought him some luck.

Twenty-four hours ago, Joe hadn't been prepared to spend money that wasn't his on a computer game. But now he was. All things considered, he felt the money owed him something.

He crossed over the road and walked into the shop. There was a large rack of *Tech Assassin* boxes facing the door, and next to it was the previous month's rave release, *Suicide Speedway*. To cap it all, his old adversary, the manager, was on duty behind the counter.

This just gets better and better, Joe thought.

The man glowered at Joe as he approached the cash desk. 'Come to waste my time on the demos again, have you?' he demanded grumpily. ' 'Cos if you have, then you can—'

Joe slapped two fifties from the wallet down on the counter. 'I'll have one *Tech Assassin* and one *Suicide Speedway*, thanks,' he said cheerfully.

He enjoyed the memory of the look on the manager's face all the way home.

Joe entered his house feeling considerably brighter than he'd felt when he left school. The two games in his bag rattled promisingly and Joe couldn't wait to try them out. He also couldn't wait to see his gran, whose little blue hatchback he had spotted parked outside his house.

'Hi, Gran!' he called as he let himself in. 'I didn't know you were coming.'

His gran and his mum were sitting in the kitchen, nursing cups of tea. They reminded him of those dolls that fit inside one another. His mum was just a younger version of her own mum – they both had similar flowery skirts, similar cardigans, and the exact same way of holding their cups of tea.

'Hello, darling,' said his gran, as he leaned down to give her a kiss on the cheek. 'I was just passing so I dropped in. Anyway . . .' she said, turning back to his mum, 'there it was, just lying on the pavement! It must have fallen out of someone's pocket.'

Joe didn't know what she was talking about, but it suddenly sounded uncomfortably familiar.

His gran noticed that he was paying attention. 'Ted, dear, my neighbour,' she explained. 'He found a mobile phone just lying in the road. There it was, brand new – and he'd almost trodden on it! Well, he took it down to the police and handed it in. Nothing happened for a couple of days, but then this stranger turns up on his doorstep with a couple of tickets for the cup final! Best seats in the stadium! The phone's owner worked there, you see, and he'd been frantic with worry about his phone, so he wanted Ted to have the tickets as a reward. Ted took his grandson to the final for his birthday and they both had a lovely time!'

'That's wonderful,' Joe's mum agreed.

'Well, you know what they say – what goes around, comes around,' Joe's gran went on, nodding wisely.

Suddenly Joe felt a lot less happy about the new games in his bag. He smiled uncomfortably. 'Yeah, I s'pose,' he said, as non-committally as he could. It wasn't just the knowledge that he hadn't been as honest as Ted that made Joe feel awkward. It was the way his gran just assumed that he would do the right thing in that situation. But, Joe reminded himself, he still intended to hand the wallet in, so surely he deserved a little good luck to balance out all the bad luck that he'd had recently.

And that meant he should start enjoying his new games as soon as possible. They weren't going to do any good just lying there in his bag. So Joe grabbed a biscuit in one hand and his bag in the other and ran upstairs.

The console in Joe's room had pride of place against one wall. It had been his special present last Christmas. He knew exactly what it must have cost and he didn't even want to think about how long his parents must have saved up for it. He had done the washing-up for a month afterwards, just to say 'thank you.' No one had asked him to, he'd just felt that it was the least he could do.

He turned it on and pressed the 'eject' button. The disc tray slid out smoothly. Then he tried to open the case for *Tech Assassin*. His fingers slipped on the cellophane wrapping. He had forgotten that new games came shrink-wrapped. That showed how often he got one.

He got out his penknife and slid the blade into the wrapping, taking care not to scratch the cover. Once he'd got the cellophane off, he prised the box open eagerly. He felt a bit like an explorer levering open an ancient tomb to reveal a priceless treasure. The disc reflected rainbow shafts of light at him as Joe laid it reverently in the disc tray. Then he sat down, the controller in his hands, poised for action.

The drive began to whirr as it read the disc. The whirring grew louder and Joe frowned. He glanced at the screen, waiting for the start-up video to show. Then the console began to shake, and Joe grew alarmed.

BANG! Joe jumped as the screen, and the console, and his bedroom light went dead. A stench of burning plastic assaulted his nose and he quickly unplugged the console from the wall. He picked it up and almost dropped it again – the plastic was too hot to touch. And when he turned the console in his hands, there was a rattling noise inside that sounded like several components had come loose.

Joe groaned as he set the console down. Despair and frustration welled up inside him. He was pretty certain that the console was a write-off. He took the disc out – that at least looked undamaged – and put it in its box. Then he shoved both games back into his bag.

'Joe?' His mum called up from downstairs. 'Are you all right? All the electric's gone off!'

'Yeah, I-I'm OK,' he shouted back, although he was feeling a bit shaken. Then he thought about what she'd said. '*All* the electric's off?' he asked.

'Looks like it,' his mum replied.

Luckily, there was enough light streaming in through the windows to see by. Joe flipped the light switch in his room, then the one out on the landing. Neither worked. But Joe knew a little about electricity and fuses and he was puzzled. He was sure that the console shouldn't have burned out like that, and it certainly shouldn't have short-circuited the entire house as well. But it had happened just as the new game was starting up, and Joe figured that was more than just coincidence.

A solid beam of light shone up the stairs. Joe's mum had found the torch. 'Mum!' he protested as she shone it right in his eyes.

'Sorry, love. Look, I'll light the way down for you,' she said, though he could see perfectly well.

'Don't worry,' Joe said, as he came downstairs. 'Look, there's a reset button in the fuse box. I'll just—'

'No, dear,' his mum interrupted firmly. 'We'll wait for your father to get home. He can do the resetting.'

'But that'll be another hour!' Joe objected. 'What about dinner?'

'Sorry, hon, no dinner until we get the power back. Anyway, it'll be nice to eat with Dad for once, won't it?'

Joe's father worked long hours and the family didn't usually get the chance to eat together.

'Great,' Joe muttered. 'Thanks!'

'Don't take that tone with me, Joe,' she said severely, and she went back into the kitchen.

But Joe hadn't been talking to her when he had said 'Thanks!' He'd been thinking about the wad of money in the wallet. He remembered all the opportunity it had represented the day before. Now, in his mind's eye, it was starting to look less like 'opportunity' and more like 'unlucky'.

Joe ran upstairs to get his bag, then grabbed his

coat from its hook by the door. 'I'm just going out for a walk,' he called.

'OK. Make sure you're back for dinner, won't you?' his mum called.

But Joe was already closing the door behind him.

Joe didn't really need the walk and it was getting dark, but he did want to clear his head. Food poisoning, a broken tooth and a ruined games console. The one thing they all had in common was the large wad of Mr Mitchell Murray's money, which right now felt like it was burning a very large hole in Joe's pocket. He wondered if the wallet's owner could somehow see what Joe was doing with his money, and was ruining it for him every step of the way. 'What goes around comes around', as his gran had said . . .

Except that Joe just didn't believe in that. *I've been bullied before*, Joe thought. *And they got away with it. No just deserts there!* He felt like he was conducting a conversation with his own conscience. *And what*

about Rob Newton? He cheated on that test and won a prize!
He couldn't stop boasting about it! And I didn't cheat and
had to sit the test again! I don't believe I'm getting all this bad
luck just because I'm spending a little money that isn't . . .

He left the thought unfinished. He had been
going to end with *rightfully mine*, but the moment
those words appeared in his mind he knew he had
lost the argument.

And, anyway, you are *getting the bad luck*, his
conscience pointed out annoyingly.

'Right, that's it,' Joe muttered aloud. 'I'm going to
the police, right now. And if anyone asks where the
missing money is, I'll just tell them that this is how
I found it. I mean, if I was going to steal it, I'd take
it all, right? I wouldn't steal a tiny bit and then hand
the rest in. So they won't think I took it.'

He walked into town, working out exactly what
he was going to say to ensure that he, Joe, appeared
completely innocent of any wrongdoing.

He reached the newsagent's where he had
bought the bar of chocolate, and scowled at it as he

passed. But then his gaze fell on an advert for the local paper which was stuck up in the window. It said: 'Bank robber killed'.

Joe kept walking, but suddenly the name Mitchell Murray caught his eye. He stopped, backed up and peered carefully through the shop window. He was sure he hadn't imagined it – something in there had Mitchell Murray's name printed on it.

And there it was. Joe saw it in the headline of the local paper: 'Dead bank robber named as Mitchell Murray.'

Joe popped into the shop, snatched up the local paper and hastily scanned the news story. 'Police have named the man killed in the car pursuit on Saturday evening as Mitchell Murray,' he read. 'Local man Murray (42) was wanted in connection with a series of robberies on bank branches in the area. His car was identified on Saturday evening by two officers on patrol and a high-speed pursuit ensued. Murray was killed instantly when his vehicle hit a lamppost at speed in Summer Hill, outside the estate agent's . . .'

Joe dropped the paper, ran out of the shop and raced round the corner into Summer Hill. When he reached the estate agent's he noticed that the lamppost outside did have a distinct bend in it, as if a car had driven into it. Joe hadn't thought much about it on Sunday because all the shutters had been down, but now he realized that the wallet had been lying right outside the estate agent's.

'Poor bloke,' Joe muttered, thinking of Mr Mitchell Murray dying in the road crash. But then the full impact of the news began to sink in. Maybe the wallet had been thrown out of the car by the force of the impact, or maybe it had fallen when the ambulance people carried Murray clear of his car. But whatever had happened, by the time Joe found the wallet, it seemed clear that its owner was already dead.

And if you're dead, Joe reasoned, *you can't own anything*. Joe felt relief flooding through him. This meant that the wallet – technically – no longer belonged to Mitchell Murray, which meant that – technically – Joe hadn't done anything wrong by spending the money! So he couldn't have earned himself the run of bad luck he'd had. That must have been nothing more than a series of unfortunate coincidences. And coincidences did happen. They were unlikely, but that was what made them coincidences.

Joe turned and headed for home, feeling a whole lot happier about everything. It was cold and dark now, and the streetlights were on, but Joe felt like he was walking on sunbeams. He reckoned he would be back just in time for his delayed dinner. His dad would have tripped the switch under the stairs and the house would have light again. Things were good.

Except that Joe couldn't help remembering why the power had gone off in the first place, and that was when the downside of his latest discovery began to occur to him. It lurked at the back of his mind like a small, dark shadow, and it grew and grew until he couldn't ignore it any longer.

The thing was, Mitchell Murray had been a bank robber. Maybe he had genuinely owned the wallet, but what about the money that was inside it? Had he genuinely owned *that*?

Maybe *Joe* hadn't stolen it from Mitchell Murray, but maybe it had *already* been stolen. In that case, Joe still had no right to be spending it like it was his own. Which meant that the food poisoning and the broken tooth and the blown console might not be coincidences after all.

'*Aagh!*' Joe growled in frustration. It seemed that whichever way he looked at it, the money wasn't his. But he would be late for dinner if he went home via the police station now. 'OK,' he announced to the night air. 'Tomorrow I'll post this wallet to the police. Then they can do what they like with it. And I'll get rid of everything I bought with the money.' Which, Joe realized, basically meant the games, because the pizza and the chocolate had already been eaten, for all the good they had done anyone. But the games had been expensive. It seemed such a waste to just chuck them away.

Joe's footsteps had led him back to the games shop and he looked up at it thoughtfully. If he could return the games and get a full refund, then he could put a lot of the money he'd spent back into the wallet. He could then send the wallet with the money – minus a few quid for the pizza and the chocolate – off to the police, and everything would be more or less as it should be.

He glanced through the door of the games shop and was pleased to see the friendly assistant on duty at the counter. He took it as a good sign and pushed the door open.

The assistant was tapping figures from receipts into a computer. 'We're just closing,' he said automatically without looking up. Then he glanced up, and grinned when he recognized Joe. 'Sorry, mate. No time for demos tonight.'

Joe swung his bag on to the counter and pulled out the games. 'I bought these here earlier,' he began.

The assistant's grin widened. 'You? Bought a game? And I missed it! Darn!'

'Yeah, but *Tech Assassin* wrecked my console,' Joe said truthfully. 'Look, I've still got the receipts. Can I just return the games for a refund?'

The man pursed his lips, though Joe could see he was sympathetic. 'Store credit only, mate, unless there's real problem. Let's see.' He popped the case of *Tech Assassin* and took out the disc, which still looked pristine and new. He slid it into a console on the counter and stood back. A moment later, the start-up logo flashed on to the screen and the theme music began to play.

'Looks OK from where I'm standing,' he said. Joe looked on yearningly as the game began. The man played it for thirty seconds, just long enough to establish that everything was fine, then ejected the disc and put it back in its box.

'I think the problem must have been with your console,' he said kindly.

'Yeah,' Joe agreed unhappily. He had a horrible feeling the problem wasn't with the console – it was a whole lot weirder than that – but he wasn't going to try to explain it now. 'Thanks,' he said, and turned and left the shop.

There was a rubbish bin on the way back home, and Joe paused in front of it for a moment, with the games in his hand. 'Can't get a refund for you,' he told them. He held them over the bin's open mouth, but somehow he still couldn't quite make himself let go. Even *stolen* money shouldn't be wasted, he thought.

And then the idea struck him like a beam of light in the dark. He would *give* the games away. Simple as that. That wouldn't be a problem, would it? Whoever got them would be completely innocent. You can't blame someone for accepting free gifts. The games had only brought *him* bad luck because of the way he had acquired them. So, a free gift was the answer.

Joe thought hard about this idea all the way home, but he couldn't see any kind of downside to it, and by the time he reached his front door he was feeling happy and relieved. Tomorrow, he vowed, he and the games would part company and he would finally get rid of all his bad luck.

The next day, Joe arrived at school, the games still in his bag. Giving the games away had seemed so simple when he had thought about it the previous evening. The hard part only occurred to him as he pushed his way through the chattering crowd that thronged the playground that morning. How do you go about handing out expensive games for free? He couldn't just shout, 'Free games!' People would think he was weird. Worse, people might be suspicious.

It occurred to Joe that no one would even know he had the games if he just kept them in his bag, so he nervously drew them out. Then he stood there, clutching the two boxes to his chest and glancing about to see if anyone had noticed.

No one had, or if they had, no one knew him well enough to realize that Joe Wright standing in the middle of the playground with nearly one hundred quid's worth of games on him was unusual.

Just then a familiar sound drew his attention. It was the rumble of skateboard wheels on concrete. The crowd parted hurriedly for Lee Hartigan as he coasted through on his board. Then he kicked the ground to get some speed up and aimed at the concrete bank that led up to the road. He scooted up into the air and flipped 180 degrees to roll back the way he had come. Lee glided to a halt and kick-stomped the board into the air, to catch it with both hands. He looked down at it and shook his head, his mouth twisted with doubt.

'Hey, Lee! Cool new board!' called one of his cronies, obviously out to suck up to him.

Lee shook his head more firmly. 'It isn't. My gran

gave it to me for my birthday, but I wish she'd asked me first 'cos I'd have told her not to get one of these. It's a good board but it doesn't suit my style. I'm going to stick with my old one.'

Lee started walking towards the school, still contemplating the board unhappily. And then he noticed Joe – or rather the copy of *Tech Assassin* Joe was still holding.

'Hey, Wright,' Lee began, his eyes fixed firmly on the games in Joe's hand. He glanced at Joe's face, then at the games again.

Joe could see Lee was torn. The struggle was visible on his face. On the one hand he was probably thinking, *It's Wright, don't want to be too friendly*. On the other hand he was clearly interested in the *Tech Assassin* game.

'Is that *Tech Assassin*?' Lee said at last, and Joe could hear the desire in his voice.

'Yeah,' Joe said, trying to sound casual. 'It's not bad.'

' "Not bad"? Are you kidding? I'm dying to get a

copy!' Lee exclaimed. 'My mum won't let me spend money on games and boards in the same month,' he added, pulling a face.

An idea popped into Joe's head and his heart pounded with sudden excitement. He hadn't been expecting this. He had just wanted to get rid of the games, but if Lee didn't want his new board . . .

'You could swap something for *Tech Assassin* if you want,' Joe said brightly. So the skateboard wasn't the right type for a master like Lee, but Joe was sure he'd be more than happy with it.

Lee looked thoughtful for a moment, but then he shrugged. 'Yeah, but all I want to get rid of is this board,' he said. 'And, no offence, but it's worth a lot more than a game, even if it *is* a pretty cool game . . .'

Joe turned his hand so that Lee could also see the copy of *Suicide Speedway*.

Lee paused. Then he said, 'Two games is different.'

'Straight swap?' Joe suggested.

Lee still looked uncertain. 'The board's still worth more . . .'

'But it's not like you paid for the board,' Joe pointed out. 'You said it was a present. I bet your gran would have given you these instead, if she'd understood.'

Lee nodded. 'Yeah,' he said, his eyes shining as he reached out to take the games. 'Yeah, OK.'

And two seconds later, Lee had two new games and Joe had a new board. One which he hadn't bought with Mitchell Murray's money, so, if there really was a curse – which, the more Joe thought about it, seemed really unlikely – then he had outwitted it. Everything had worked out better than he could possibly have hoped.

It was going to be a good day at school.

It was hard to concentrate on lessons with an almost brand-new skateboard in his locker. What made it even harder to concentrate was the fact that Kate had returned to class. Joe took it as a good sign. He was doing the right thing with the money and already things were looking up.

Kate was sitting just in front of him, but she didn't look in his direction. Joe couldn't tell if she was annoyed with him or just busy, but he hoped they could still be friends.

He didn't get much opportunity to talk to her during the rest of the day, and the few times it looked like a chance might occur, he didn't quite have the nerve to make the most of it. He figured that if she was still getting over food poisoning, she might not be in the mood to chat with the boy who gave it to her.

The long school day finally drew to an end and the skateboard was waiting for him. Joe took it out of his locker self-consciously. The corridor was packed with fellow students all in a hurry to get home. Joe was pretty sure that no one would give him a second glance, but he decided he wasn't going to try to ride the board in the playground with everyone else around. He knew he wasn't exactly an expert and he didn't want to end up flat on his back with half the school looking on.

So Joe walked home with the board under his arm, and waited until school was well out of sight before trying his luck. Then he laid the skateboard carefully down on the pavement and rested one foot on top. He gave a shove with the other foot and suddenly he was moving.

'Woohoo!' he yelled. Then the board wobbled and he almost came off, so Joe stopped and tried to picture Lee when he was boarding. How did the other boy stand?

Lee stands with both feet wide apart . . . Joe thought. He put one foot in line with the board, kicked off with the other foot and then stood with it across the back of the board, as he remembered Lee doing.

He was moving at a snail's pace now, but he felt stable and it was surprisingly easy.

What else does Lee do? Joe thought eagerly. *Ah, yes* . . .

He kicked off again and this time he crouched down a little, lowering his centre of gravity. As far as Joe could remember, Lee seemed to balance by moving his hips from side to side. So Joe tried to imitate the other boy, and suddenly he found that he was really doing it. He was heading down the pavement at a steady pace, with the wheels thrumming beneath him and the wind ruffling his hair. This was it. He was actually skateboarding!

Up ahead, the pavement curved as it followed the road round to the left.

How do I steer? Joe thought frantically. *Help!*

Desperately, Joe shifted his balance a little, moving his hips like Lee, and the board smoothly took the bend. Joe straightened up again and whooped with glee.

It occurred to him suddenly that he was getting near to the park with its skateboarding ramps. He hadn't intended to go there until he was a bit better at boarding, but he was pleased with his progress and he wanted to give the ramps a try. No one would expect him to be in the Lee Hartigan class, he told himself. But he would be there, part of the boarding scene – if only a small part – and it would be cool.

He needed to cross the road to get to the park, so he scooted as far as the traffic lights and hopped off before he pressed the button. He waited for the lights to change, with one foot on the ground and the other resting on the board. Suddenly, the skateboard rolled forward a couple of centimetres, making Joe stumble into the road. He quickly regained his balance and jumped backwards just as a lorry sped past, right in front of him. *OK,* Joe thought, *I'm still pretty new at this. I'll have to be more careful.*

Once on the other side of the road, he jumped back on his board. He found that as long as he kept an eye on the ups and downs ahead of him, and stayed well away from the kerb, it was easy and fun. Joe cruised through the gates of the park and headed down the main path towards the skateboarding ramps.

'Joe!' A familiar voice called his name and he staggered to an abrupt halt. He hadn't expected to see Kate at the park, but there she was, smiling and looking pleased to see him.

'Kate, hi!' he said. 'Um . . . how are you? I mean, I'm really sorry about that stupid pizza and . . .' Joe trailed off, not really sure what more he could say.

'Yeah, well, I've decided to forgive you!' Kate replied, with a grin that showed she didn't bear him any ill-will. 'It wasn't your fault. It's not like *you* cooked it, or anything. And I'm OK now.' She rubbed her stomach carefully. 'As long as I don't eat much. Nice board,' she went on, changing the subject. 'I didn't know you had one.'

'Oh, I'm just a beginner,' Joe said quickly. 'I mean, I can roll along but that's about it.'

Kate laughed. 'That's more than I can do!' she said. 'I come off after about half a second. Go on, show me.'

'Well . . .' Joe was torn between the desire to show Kate that he was already pretty good and the fear that maybe it was all a fluke and he would come off and land on his head in front of her. The urge to show off a little won. 'All right,' he said, and kicked off to roll in a wide circle all round her.

Kate applauded. 'That's great!' she declared. 'Look, I was going to meet up with the guys. Come with me.'

'Oh, well, I really . . .' Joe began, but she was already heading off to the board area, assuming he would follow, so he figured he'd better go with her. Besides, that was where he'd been heading for anyway.

They chatted as they made their way towards the ramps, and Joe began to feel more at ease. Up ahead he could see Lee doing his stuff. He heard a familiar shout of 'Five-forty!' and Lee flew up into the air above the heads of his admirers.

'Bet you can't do that,' Kate said, but she laughed

when she said it and Joe knew she wasn't meaning to tease.

He grinned back. 'Not yet!'

Lee landed again and coasted to a halt.

'Hey, Lee!' Kate shouted. 'Show us how you do that.'

'It's easy,' Lee said, skating over to join them. 'You just start with a simple one-eighty and build up from there.'

'Yeah, easy,' Joe said doubtfully. He was fairly sure that 'starting with a simple one-eighty' wasn't within his range.

'Go on, give it a try,' Lee urged. He seemed quite friendly. Maybe he was still feeling grateful for the games. 'Look, I'll go through it with you,' Lee offered. And to his surprise, Joe found himself being led over to the starting point.

Joe stood on his board while Lee demonstrated.

'Watch,' Lee said. 'You kick off like this . . .' He pushed off with his foot, and Joe did likewise.

It was meant to be a careful, tentative push, but

Joe suddenly found himself shooting towards the ramp. He just had time to see Lee's look of surprise as he flew past, and then he was too busy worrying about the approaching ramp to think about anything else.

Joe realized that he had a choice of leaping off and looking stupid or trying to take the jump. He definitely didn't want to look stupid in front of Kate, so he decided to try to cope with the ramp. The board hit the curved surface and shot up into the air. Joe clenched his teeth and braced himself for the inevitable fall.

Except that he felt his body shifting with the board. His centre of gravity was moving. Joe flexed his knees and crouched over to find that he and the board were turning in midair at exactly the same speed, so that they came down together. Suddenly he was back on the ground again, coasting away from the ramp with a successful one-eighty behind him.

'All *right*!' shouted Lee in amazement. 'Joe's got it!'

Joe felt hugely proud and ridiculously happy. He could feel an enormous grin on his face and exhilaration blazed inside him. The other ramp was approaching and before he could chicken out, he decided to go for it one more time.

He hit the ramp and flew up into the air again, and again he felt his body adjusting. It was like the board was glued to his feet as they turned together . . . and kept turning . . .

Alarm bells went off inside Joe's head. He had gone too far! He was way past the one-eighty! He was going to fall! But he *kept* turning, another full circle, and then he was back on the ground with the board firmly beneath his feet. Unbelievably, he had done a five-forty! Even Lee had never done better than that!

Kate, Lee and Lee's admirers stared in disbelief for a few seconds, and then started cheering.

OK, Joe thought, *time to quit while I'm ahead*. He braced his feet to slow the board down, but nothing happened. Panic flooded through him.

How was he going to stop? He was going much too fast to just put his foot down.

Suddenly the skateboard swerved over to the right, away from the ramp. Joe saw a metal bar ahead, like a stair rail. The sight of that made him swallow his pride and try to jump off the board, but his feet wouldn't move. He opened his mouth to yell, and then somehow he had stomped down on the board and it had soared up into the air, and twisted. It hit the rail sideways on and he slid down it, perfectly balanced with a foot on either side. Almost before he knew it, he had landed safely on the ground at the end of the rail.

Everyone was cheering now, and clapping their hands in time with his name. 'Joe! Joe! Joe!'

'It's not me!' Joe shouted helplessly, but he realized that they couldn't hear him.

And now the board was heading back to the ramp. He shot up the slope, landed right on the rim and spun round twice on his rear wheels, then shot back down to the ground again.

Joe wasn't even trying to seem brave now. 'Help me! Get me off this thing!' he screamed in terror.

But the board had something else in mind. It shot off again and hit the ramp at an angle, so that Joe flew up sideways, away from the ramp.

And then time slowed down. Joe felt like he was hanging in the air for a very long time. Ahead of him he could see the swings and roundabouts of the kiddie play area next to the board park. And in his mind's eye, he could see the path he was taking through the air. It ended right in the middle of the climbing frame. There was nothing he could do about it.

Below him the cheers had dried up, swallowed by a horrified silence. Then someone started screaming. It might have been Joe.

And then time sped up again to its usual rate, and Joe crashed into the climbing frame. There was a brief moment of searing agony, a feeling of shattering and breaking.

He couldn't move.

The whole world was receding down a long dark tunnel. And waiting for him in the darkness was a man Joe had never seen before. But, somehow, Joe knew who he was: Mr Mitchell Murray, grinning cruelly as he tucked a wallet full of money into his pocket.

Terrify yourself with more books from Nick Shadow's
Midnight Library

Vol. I: *Voices*

Kate knows that something is wrong when she starts hearing voices in her head. But she doesn't know what the voices mean, or what terror they will lead her to . . .

Vol. II: *Blood and Sand*

John and Sarah are on the most boring seaside holiday of their lives. And when they come up against the sinister Sandman, they really begin to wish they'd stayed at home . . .

Vol. III: *End Game*

Simon is a computer addict. When he's sent a mysterious new game, the lines between virtual reality and real life become terrifyingly blurred . . .

Terrify yourself with more books from Nick Shadow's
Midnight Library

Vol. IV: *The Cat Lady*

Chloe never quite believed her friend's stories about the Cat Lady. But when a dare goes horribly wrong, she finds out that the truth is more terrifying than anyone had ever imagined . . .

Vol. V: *Liar*

Lauren is shy. She just wants a friend, and she's so lonely she even imagined herself one. But she soon realizes she's created a monster. A monster called Jennifer . . .

Vol. VI: *Shut your Mouth*

Louise and her mates love to get their sweets from Mr Webster's old-fashioned shop, but when their plan to get some of the new 'Special Delights' goes wrong, could they have bitten off more than they can chew?

Terrify yourself with more books from Nick Shadow's
Midnight Library

Vol. VII: *I Can See You*
Michael didn't want to move out of the city in the first place. And wandering round the countryside in the dark really isn't his idea of fun – particularly when he finds out how dangerous the dark can be . . .

Vol. VIII: *The Catch*
David and Adam aren't too worried when they get lost on the open sea. But when they discover an abandoned boat in the fog, things start to turn nasty. Who – or *what* – lies in wait beyond the waves . . . ?

Vol. IX: *The Whisperer*
Rachael has always wanted to be a journalist, so writing for the student paper is a perfect opportunity. But then her column begins to write itself, and soon no subject is safe . . .